Dear Harlequin Intrigue Reader,

You may be surprised to find me and the Randalls in the Harlequin Intrigue line. Normally my books are not filled with murder and mayhem. However, I couldn't resist the opportunity to give one of my Randalls the chance to play a real hero. Jim Randall, Chad and Megan's oldest boy, has been drifting since he completed college. When a call for help from a former flame arouses old memories, he finds he can't abandon Patience Anderson. He plays the role of hero very well, but his emotions aren't as easily directed. I hope you like his story.

The Randalls always pull together to bring about a happy ending. This remarkable family won't have it any other way. There are, of course, some rough moments, but the Randalls face every test, fearlessly doing what has to be done. We can't always choose our paths in life, but we can control our behavior.

It was interesting for me to accompany my characters through a different kind of story, one of danger and escape. I hope you enjoy the change, and I promise I will return to Rawhide and the Randalls once again this December.

Best wishes,

Judy Christenberry

Dear Harlequin Intrigue Reader,

Beginning this October, Harlequin Intrigue has expanded its lineup to *six* books! Publishing two more titles each month enables us to bring you an extraordinary selection of breathtaking stories of romantic suspense filled with exciting editorial variety—and we encourage you to try all that we have to offer.

Stock up on catnip! Caroline Burnes brings back your favorite feline sleuth to beckon you into a new mystery in the popular series FEAR FAMILIAR. This four-legged detective sticks his whiskers into the mix to help clear a stunning stuntwoman's name in *Familiar Double*. Up next is Dani Sinclair's new HEARTSKEEP trilogy starting with *The Firstborn*—a darkly sensual gothic romance that revolves around a sinister suspense plot. To lighten things up, bestselling Harlequin American Romance author Judy Christenberry crosses her beloved BRIDES FOR BROTHERS series into Harlequin Intrigue with *Randall Renegade*—a riveting reunion romance that will keep you on the edge of your seat.

Keeping Baby Safe by Debra Webb could either passionately reunite a duty-bound COLBY AGENCY operative and his onetime lover—or tear them apart forever. Don't miss the continuation of this action-packed series. Then Amy J. Fetzer launches our BACHELORS AT LARGE promotion featuring fearless men in blue with *Under His Protection*. Finally, watch for *Dr. Bodyguard* by debut author Jessica Andersen. Will a hunky doctor help penetrate the emotional walls around a lady genius before a madman closes in?

Pick up all six for a complete reading experience you won't forget!

Enjoy,

Denise O'Sullivan
Senior Editor
Harlequin Intrigue

RANDALL RENEGADE

JUDY CHRISTENBERRY

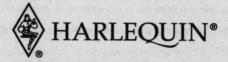

HARLEQUIN®

TORONTO • NEW YORK • LONDON
AMSTERDAM • PARIS • SYDNEY • HAMBURG
STOCKHOLM • ATHENS • TOKYO • MILAN • MADRID
PRAGUE • WARSAW • BUDAPEST • AUCKLAND

ISBN 0-373-22731-0

RANDALL RENEGADE

Copyright © 2003 by Judy Russell Christenberry

Visit us at www.eHarlequin.com

Printed in U.S.A.

ABOUT THE AUTHOR

Judy Christenberry has been writing romances for fifteen years because she loves happy endings as much as her readers. A former French teacher, Judy now devotes herself to writing full-time. She hopes readers have as much fun reading her stories as she does writing them. She spends her spare time reading, watching her favorite sports teams and keeping track of her two daughters. Judy is a native Texan.

Books by Judy Christenberry

THE RANDALLS

THE RANDALL BROTHERS

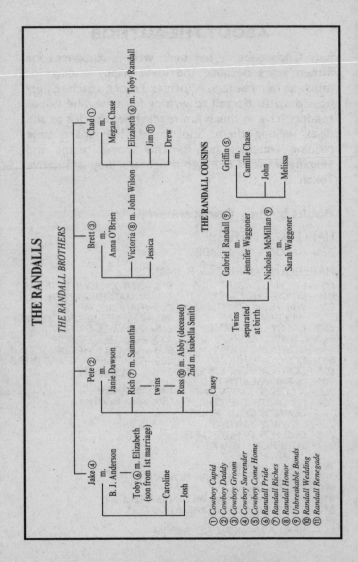

Jake ④
m.
B. J. Anderson
Toby ⑥ m. Elizabeth
(son from 1st marriage)
— Caroline
— Josh

Pete ②
m.
Janie Dawson
— Rich ⑦ m. Samantha
— twins
— Russ ⑩ m. Abby (deceased)
2nd m. Isabella Smith
— Casey

Brett ③
m.
Anna O'Brien
— Victoria ⑧ m. John Wilson
— Jessica

Chad ①
m.
Megan Chase
— Elizabeth ⑥ m. Toby Randall
— Jim ⑪
— Drew

THE RANDALL COUSINS

Gabriel Randall ⑨
m.
Jennifer Waggoner

Nicholas McMillan ⑨
m.
Sarah Waggoner

Twins separated at birth

Griffin ⑤
m.
Camille Chase
— John
— Melissa

① *Cowboy Cupid*
② *Cowboy Daddy*
③ *Cowboy Groom*
④ *Cowboy Surrender*
⑤ *Cowboy Come Home*
⑥ *Randall Pride*
⑦ *Randall Riches*
⑧ *Randall Honor*
⑨ *Unbreakable Bonds*
⑩ *Randall Wedding*
⑪ *Randall Renegade*

CAST OF CHARACTERS

Jim Randall—A man of honor who can't say no to a voice from the past.

Patience Anderson—The fiercely protective mother has no one else to turn to.

Chad Randall—His beloved son wants to stand alone, but that's not the Randall way.

Joseph Keats—His fanatical beliefs have already cost his wife her life. Will his son also pay the ultimate price?

Tommy Peters—A little boy who loves and trusts Patience, the only mother he's ever known. Can he trust her to rescue him?

For Pat Bennett:
first a devoted fan, now a good friend.

Chapter One

Jim Randall presented himself in the kitchen at dinnertime because it was expected. But he wasn't staying. "Red, I'm heading into town. Don't count me in for dinner."

"You're supposed to let me know earlier, boy. You got something special planned?" the older man asked.

"Not really, Red. I'm meeting a few friends. Sorry I didn't know this morning."

As he turned away, his father, Chad Randall, entered the big kitchen, and Jim had to explain himself all over again. And if he didn't hurry out, his mom would be next. As much as he loved his family, twenty-five seemed a little old to be tied so tightly to the apron strings.

"Wait, boy," Red said. "You got a phone message. Sounded real important." Red handed him a piece of paper.

Jim scanned the message, and his heart jerked. He carefully folded it and said, "Thanks, Red."

Red wasn't finished. "The girl on the phone was crying."

Damn! Why couldn't the old man mind his own business? Jim felt badly immediately. Red was like a grandfather to him. He loved him. But he didn't want anyone asking any questions about the call.

His father looked at him, but didn't say anything. Jim knew that his father would lend help if it was needed, and he gave him a rocky smile as he hurried out of the kitchen.

He climbed into his truck and headed toward the county road that led into Rawhide, one of the small towns splattered across Wyoming. He'd been born there, knew most everyone who lived there, and he played there on Friday nights.

He stopped halfway to town, pulling over to the side of the road. He turned on the overhead light as he drew the piece of paper out of his pocket. Patience Anderson.

He ground his teeth as images flew before his eyes. He'd fallen for her hard. They'd both been at the University of Wyoming in Laramie. It had been his senior year, her sophomore. He'd wanted her badly. She'd refused to sleep with him unless they were at least engaged.

Jim hadn't been ready to settle down. He wanted to sow his wild oats and make a name for himself first. It wasn't easy being a Randall in the state of Wyoming. His family was well-known in the ranching and rodeo communities. So he'd said no to getting engaged so young. In actual fact, he'd said, "Hell, no!"

After two weeks without Patience, he'd realized he'd made a mistake. He missed her terribly. When he'd gone back home for a weekend, he went into town to see his friends and catch up on the news. The first thing his friends told him was that Patience was raising a baby. It wasn't hers, really, but she was going to raise it.

Jim had torn out of the saloon and found a pay phone. He called Patience. Her voice was cool when she'd told him that yes, she was raising a baby.

"Who's the real mother and father?" he'd demanded.

"None of your business," she'd said.

"Fine!" and he'd hung up the phone.

He hadn't seen or heard from her since. It had been three years, but she still owned his heart whether she knew it or not.

And now she had called him. She'd cried on the phone, asked him to call back. What was going on?

He started his truck and drove fast to Rawhide. He went to the same pay phone he'd used to call her before. He didn't need to look at the paper. He still knew her number by heart. Not that he'd ever tell her that.

"Hello?" a wavery voice answered.

"Patience?" he asked. After all, Red had said she was crying.

"No, I'll get her."

He grew even more tense as he waited.

"Jim?"

"Yeah."

He didn't intend to make this call easy for her. He'd suffered a lot because she'd wanted nothing to do with him unless they were engaged.

"I need help. I didn't know anyone else to call."

"What kind of help?"

"My little boy has been kidnapped."

"And you haven't called the law?"

"I called them."

"Then why are you asking me for help?"

"They won't do anything."

Jim was momentarily speechless. "Why not?" he finally asked.

"Because the man who kidnapped him is his father!" The tears were there in her voice.

"Sounds like you'd better listen to the law, Patience."

"You don't understand! He's crazy!"

"No, I don't understand. And I don't know why you're coming to me for help. You threw me out of your life years ago!"

"*I* threw *you* out of *my* life?" she screamed back at him.

"That's right. Find someone else to fight your battles."

He hung up the phone.

After an hour of sitting at a back table in the saloon having a beer with his friends, he asked, "What do you hear about Patience now?"

"Nothin'," his friend Roy said. Roy worked at the feed store and knew almost all the gossip around.

"Nothing? Does she still have that kid?"

"Last I saw her she did."

"Who's she seeing now?"

Roy shrugged. "Maybe someone from Buffalo."

"I see. Well, good. Glad she's happy."

Another half an hour and he made an excuse and headed for his truck. Of course Patience was seeing someone. She was a beautiful woman. So let her ask her new boyfriend for help.

AFTER A RESTLESS night, Jim rose and grabbed the phone in the bachelor pad, which was what the bunkhouse built for him and his cousins was called. It was early, but he figured Patience would be awake.

The same wavery voice answered.

"May I speak to Patience?"

"No. She's gone."

"Is this Mrs. Anderson?" Patience's mother hadn't sounded this old three years ago.

"Yes."

"This is Jim Randall. When will Patience be back?"

"I don't know. She went to find Tommy."

"Is that her son? The one she said was taken?"

"Yes," the woman said with a sob. "Patience has gone after Tommy and I'm so afraid the boy's father will hurt them."

"Mrs. Anderson, I'm coming over to see you. I'll be there in about half an hour." He hung up before the woman could say yes or no.

Jim knocked on his little brother's door in the bachelor pad, then stuck his head in. "Drew, tell Dad I had some personal business to take care of. I'll get back as soon as I can."

"What time is it?" Drew asked, rubbing his eyes. He'd finished university last year and still wasn't happy with the early mornings.

"Almost six. Tell Dad, okay?"

Drew closed his eyes and nodded at the same time. Jim didn't hold out much hope that he'd remember.

When Jim reached the small brick home on one of the few back streets of Rawhide, he parked his truck and hurried to the front door. Knocking, he called, "Mrs. Anderson? It's Jim Randall. Can you let me in?"

The door opened slowly. A woman he remembered as vibrant appeared pale and worn as she peered at him through the screen. Slowly she pushed it open and gestured for him to enter.

"Mrs. Anderson, I need to know what has happened to Patience. You said she's gone after her little boy? Won't that be dangerous?"

"Yes. I told her not to go. But she wouldn't listen to me."

"Where did she go?"

"Up in the mountains. The boy's father has a

camp up there. He…he just came to our house and grabbed the boy. And he cleaned out our pantry and left some worthless coins in place of the groceries.''

Jim frowned. ''What do you mean, worthless coins?''

The woman hurried to a pine dresser. She picked up something and returned to Jim.

''These,'' she said as she poured five small tin disks into his hand.

''Did you show them to the sheriff?'' he asked.

''What's the point? He already said he wouldn't help us.''

''Why?''

''Because we never did anything legally about Tommy. Patience never formally adopted him. Legally, Joseph, his father, has custody.''

''Why do you think he's dangerous?''

''Because he's crazy. He wants Tommy to be a soldier!''

''And you told the sheriff this?''

''He told us he couldn't do anything.''

Jim was as frustrated as Patience's mother sounded. ''I'll go talk to the sheriff.''

''But what about Patience and Tommy?'' She

gave him a pleading look, tears streaming down her cheeks.

Awkwardly he patted her arm. "I'll do what I can." He turned and left.

A sharp wind was blowing and he settled his hat on his head and turned up his collar. It was late October and it wasn't unusual to have northers blow through, some of them with snow.

He parked in front of the sheriff's office. Jim knew Sheriff Metzger well. He'd had one or two minor run-ins with the law as a teenager, but he'd become a model citizen.

"Sheriff Metzger," he said as he entered, sticking out his hand.

"Jim, how are you?"

"Fine. I have some questions, though."

"Well, sure, son. Come on in and have a seat. How about some coffee?"

"Thanks. I'd like that." Jim settled into the chair beside the sheriff's desk. He glanced at the only other man in the office, an elderly deputy. "Hi, Dick. How's it going?"

"Just fine, Jim. Tell your daddy hello for me."

"Sure."

The sheriff set down a mug of coffee beside

Jim and circled the desk to take a seat. "Now, then, what's bothering you?"

"It's about Patience Anderson. She's an old friend and—"

Sheriff Metzger held up a hand. "I told her I couldn't help her," he said.

"Sheriff, I talked to Patience briefly last night. But her mother says she left to go after the boy and I'm—"

"She left? Surely she hasn't gone up to Kane's camp! I told her she'd just have to wait. He'll get tired of a little boy, I said. He won't want to take care of him."

"Who is this man?"

"You don't know? Do you remember Faith, Patience's older sister? She married a man named Joseph Kane. When Faith died—"

"Faith is dead?" Jim asked, shocked. He hadn't heard anything about that. He would've called Patience if he'd known...

"I thought you said Patience was a friend."

"She was. But apart from last night, I haven't talked to her in three years. What happened to Faith?"

"She died in childbirth. That husband of hers didn't want her to see a doctor. She bled to death. The baby was saved because Patience got there in time to get him to the doctor.''

"So she's raising her sister's baby?"

"Yeah," the sheriff said, rubbing his chin. "I wish I could help her, but by law, Kane has rights to the boy."

"So he's living in the mountains? At a camp, not in a house?"

"Right. He's camped out with his men."

"His men?" Jim asked.

"He's got himself a group of followers, 'soldiers' he calls them. But so far, they've kept to themselves. And we're short-handed here. Otherwise, I'd go talk to the man. But I wouldn't go alone, and it'd take us a couple of days to get there."

"Is he violent?"

"Don't know. But I don't like being completely outnumbered. That's why I told that little lady to give it some time. I can't believe she went after him. Why, the weather alone could kill her. There's a storm coming."

"Can you give me directions? I need to make sure Patience is all right."

"Well, I'll give you the information I have."

An hour later, after visiting Mrs. Anderson briefly to tell her he'd try to check up on Patience, he headed back to his family's ranch. He had some preparing to do.

Megan, Jim's mother, was sitting with Red at the big kitchen table, coffee cups in front of them, when he walked in.

"Where you been, boy?" Red immediately asked.

"I wanted to talk to Patience. She was the one who called me yesterday. I found out she may be in some trouble. Where's Dad?"

"He went with your uncle Pete to deliver some bulls to Cheyenne. They were going to stay overnight and visit with some other customers."

Jim didn't need an explanation. His uncle Pete had run his business for a number of years, supplying animals for rodeos. But that meant he couldn't discuss things with his dad. Well, he *had* been complaining about Red treating him like a child. Here was an opportunity to make his own decisions.

"Red, could you rustle me up some breakfast? I'm starving." He knew he'd need food to eat before he set out. "And then I'm going after Patience."

"Where is she?" his mother asked.

"Up in the mountains. By the way, did you hear about her sister Faith's death?"

"Yes, of course. Your aunt Anna was terribly distressed about it. Especially since Faith's life could've been saved."

"Patience is raising her sister's boy."

"Of course she is. I'm sorry the two of you broke up. She's a wonderful person." Megan cast a look at him. Then she asked, "Why is Patience up in the mountains?"

"The boy's father took him up there. Patience has gone after him."

"Did she call the sheriff?"

"Yeah. But it seems that the man is within his rights. Patience doesn't have legal guardianship of the boy."

"Oh, no," Megan said. "Poor Patience."

"Yeah."

"Who's going with you?"

Jim was distracted by the plate of scrambled eggs and bacon Red set in front of him, along with a big glass of milk.

"Thanks, Red. Looks great."

"Jim? Who are you taking with you?" his mother asked with more urgency.

"I'm going by myself. I'm just going to convince Patience there's nothing she can do if the man wants his son."

"But exactly where are you going?" Megan persisted.

"I've got directions from the sheriff. I know what I'm doing, Mom."

"But there's a storm brewing. I heard it could be bad."

"That's why I need to be on my way. I need to get out of the foothills before the storm comes. I'll be all right."

He'd been eating while she questioned him, and now he finished the milk and stood. "I'm changing clothes, grabbing some supplies, and then I'm on my way." He leaned down and kissed his mother's cheek. "I'll take the walkie-talkie with me. I'll be in contact for a while, anyway."

"Be careful, son."

"I will, Mom. Oh, by the way, when the boy's father took the kid, he left some of these worthless coins." Jim handed her one. "I think it's made of tin."

"What does the 'p' stand for?" Megan asked.

"Your guess is as good as mine." He kissed her again, and hurried to get his things together.

THE RIDE ON HORSEBACK up the mountain was taking much longer than he'd anticipated, but Patience was at least half a day ahead of him and he wanted to make up time. He'd found some signs of her earlier, but the new snow obliterated everything now.

He finally made camp underneath a rocky overhang, which provided shelter for him and his horse from the snow and wind. After building a small fire to heat some coffee and toast the sandwich Red had packed for him, he fed the horse and unfurled his bedroll.

It didn't take long for him to fall asleep. But he found himself waking to nightmares in which he was unable to save Patience.

When a nightmare woke him for the third time, it was four-thirty, and he decided to give up sleeping.

He broke camp half an hour later. The sun still wasn't up and he had to go slowly. Snow was still falling, but the farther he moved up the mountain, the less snow there was on the ground. That would continue to be true until he hit the tree line. According to the sheriff's directions, the camp was near the tree line. So he'd know when he was getting closer by the amount of snow.

He was preparing to stop again for the night when he thought he heard something.

He reined in his horse and listened, but was met with silence. Then his horse nickered softly. "Easy, boy," Jim whispered.

He still heard nothing but decided to go on a little farther. The sheriff had told him to turn north when he was close to the tree line. He'd also warned him to approach Kane and his men cautiously.

Jim had taken the warning seriously. He'd hidden a small pistol in one boot and a knife in the other. He also wore a gun and had a rifle on his saddle, but they might take any visible weapons.

He hoped not. He wanted to handle this situation peaceably. He only hoped Patience would cooperate. He'd always teased her that she didn't live up to her name. She had a quick temper that matched the red streaks in her blond hair.

Jim brought himself up short. He didn't need to think about Patience's temper or her beautiful hair. He needed to focus on what was important.

Which he did.

And then he heard a woman scream.

Chapter Two

"I told you to stand at attention!" Joseph Kane yelled at the little boy crumpled in the snow, sobbing against Patience's leg.

"Stop this!" Patience yelled. "He's not even three yet." Dear God, if she didn't get her nephew out of here quickly, he'd die at his crazy father's hand. How had her sister ever loved this man?

Faith had died because of him, and Patience wasn't about to leave Tommy to the same fate. He was such a good little boy, so well behaved and loving. He was even already learning to read. And Kane had struck him because he couldn't stand at attention for an hour at a time. It was outrageous!

"He's too young to play soldier," she told Joseph.

"Because you spoil him. He's my son. He will do as I say!"

Tommy shivered against her and Patience knew it wasn't from the cold. He was terrified. She crouched down and hugged him. She had no idea how she was going to get them out of here.

She knew Joseph Kane wasn't ready to give up his child. By the time she'd arrived at the camp, however, Tommy had been abused both physically and mentally. Kane's brutality was already changing Tommy's open, loving nature. Oh, how she hated Kane.

But that wasn't anything new. Her sister's death had instilled in her a hatred for this man that had never gone away. Faith had been so gentle and kind. And that monster had taken advantage of her goodness.

"Go to your tent, Patience!" Kane commanded.

"Only if Tommy goes with me. He's cold and tired. He needs to rest."

"I am the general. You do not argue with me!"

She stood up with the little boy in her arms. "All right. I won't." She started to walk to the tent Kane had assigned her.

She certainly had no interest in arguing with Kane—or any of his men. When she'd arrived last night, she'd studied them, hoping to find an ally. But all of Kane's followers were loyal to him. His three "lieutenants" were cruel, hard men, just like Joseph.

"Woman, put down that child!" he yelled.

"I'm going to our tent, just as you said, *General*." She knew she should try to keep the sarcasm out of her voice, but it was impossible.

"Not with the boy!" She heard the heavy tread of feet behind her and quickened her pace.

"Hey, there!"

Everyone, including Patience, turned to look at the man who had called to the general. In the dusk she couldn't make out his face. He and his horse were being led into camp by a pair of guards. Another guard followed with a rifle pointed at the man.

"Who are you?" Kane demanded.

"Jim Bradford."

Patience froze. That was Jim Randall's voice. He'd come after her! Fear swept through her. Kane would kill him.

"Why are you here, Mr. Bradford?" Kane asked.

"I was riding on the trail and I heard a lady

scream,'' Jim replied. ''I thought she needed help.''

Patience, holding Tommy tightly to her, was waiting to see what would happen. Jim looked straight at her.

''Ma'am, do you need some help?''

Yes! Oh, yes, I do! She shook her head.

Jim actually reached up and tipped his hat to her. ''My mistake, ma'am.''

''So you'll be on your way,'' Kane said coldly.

''Well, if I were in a hurry, I guess I would, but I'm not. I've decided I don't much like society anymore… Hey, I sure could use a cup of coffee.'' He stared pointedly at the coffeepot beside the fire.

Kane hesitated. ''Okay. And you can stay here tonight if you want. But we'll keep your weapons until you leave. You have a problem with that?''

''Nope. I didn't catch your name.''

One of his lieutenants answered for Kane. ''He's the general of our troops. You address him as General.''

Patience knew how pretentious Jim would think the title. Counting Kane himself, the camp had fewer than twenty men. Not exactly a lot of troops.

"Well, thank you, General, for your hospitality," Jim said. "I'd like to ask you some questions about where a man could winter up here and come out better than a chunk of ice."

"We'll talk after dinner," Kane said slowly, watching the newcomer.

Patience took Kane's momentary distraction with the stranger as an opportunity to slip into her small tent. Sinking down on the canvas floor, she kissed Tommy's cheek. "You were very brave, sweetheart. Mommy is so proud of you."

"I don't like him," Tommy whispered, sniffing.

Patience found a tissue to wipe the boy's nose. "I know, sweetheart. But we may be able to get away and go back home to Grandma."

"Grandma will miss me," Tommy said.

"Oh, yes, she will." Tommy was right. Since her older daughter's death, only Tommy had brought smiles to her mother's face. Patience had hated to leave her alone, but rescuing Tommy from the likes of Joseph Kane was of prime importance.

"I'm hungry, Mommy."

Patience reached into her knapsack and pulled

out a small candy bar. "That's because you didn't have any lunch. But supper will be in a little while."

"Will he let us eat?"

"I hope so. If he doesn't, I have more candy."

"I want to stay in here," Tommy declared. "I don't mind eating candy."

Patience chuckled. It was a relief to release some of her tension. "I can tell you don't mind," she said.

"Ma'am?"

Patience stilled as a man stuck his head through the tent opening. To her relief, it wasn't Kane, but Roger, one of his less-vicious followers. "Yes?"

"The general requests your presence for dinner in his tent," Roger stated.

"What about Tommy?"

"Uh, I'll…I'll bring him dinner here in the tent if you want."

"That would be very nice, Roger. Will you stay and eat with him? And remain with him until I return?"

"Uh, I'll do what I can, ma'am. He…he reminds me of my little brother."

"Thank you, Roger. I appreciate your kindness. Will dinner include anyone else?"

"Yes, ma'am. The triplets," he said, using the nickname for the lieutenants, "and our visitor."

"All right, Roger. Thank you."

"Yes, ma'am," he said, closing the tent flap as he left.

She closed her eyes for a moment, thinking about what was before her. Dinner with Jim. He'd come to save them, she was certain. It was the first ray of hope she'd felt since she'd set off to retrieve her son.

She was thrilled that Jim had come after her. He was still the good guy she remembered. Like everyone in his family, he did what was right, no matter the cost to him.

JIM LOOKED UP as Patience entered the large tent the general called home. He'd spent the past hour pretending to be a man who was fed up with society. He'd even hinted at having had trouble with the law.

That had pleased the general.

To his surprise, the general stood and extended his hand to Patience. She ignored the gesture and sat on the only vacant camp stool.

"Jim, this is Patience, another guest tonight."

He turned to her. "My dear, we mustn't let our little differences give our guest the wrong idea."

She heard the warning beneath the false words and remained silent.

Kane nodded to one of his lieutenants and the man slipped from the tent. His mission became clear as several of the soldiers brought in food. To Jim's surprise, the main dish was steaks, cooked to perfection.

"You eat well, General. I didn't expect such quality in a camp meal."

"Steaks are the easy part. It's the vegetables that are hard to come by. The steaks are generously donated by the ranchers in the area, though sometimes I pay."

Jim remembered the coins in his jeans pocket. Were they what Kane considered payment? Now he knew where some of the Randalls' missing cattle had gone.

"I'm hoping to find someplace cut off, but with a source of supplies not too far away," Jim said, continuing his pretense of wanting a place to hide away.

The general leaned forward, his focus on Jim. "I understand. I wonder if you might consider joining us. I supply all my men's needs. You might stay for the winter and see if you agree with our mission.''

"What is your mission, General?''

Kane gave a mournful sigh. "I fear citizens are misled by their Christian leaders. I believe the prize goes to the fittest. I intend to rule Wyoming."

"That would be hard to do unless you dismantled the government, wouldn't it?''

"Ah, my friend, you are quick. I don't intend to dismantle it. I intend to rule it. I shall be elected governor."

It was tempting to laugh at the man. As far as Jim could tell, Kane had formed an army only to wait on him. He didn't look prepared to overthrow anyone, much less run for office.

Jim risked a glance at Patience to see what she thought of the general's plan. Their gazes met and she immediately turned away. He watched her look at the general before she turned her attention to her food.

He suspected the vegetables were the ones stolen from her mother's pantry. But Patience remained cool. In control. That was what the situation required, but the Patience he remembered hadn't been good at holding back.

Obviously she'd matured.

"So what do you think?" the general asked. "Care to join our crusade?"

"I wouldn't mind wintering with you, but I can't promise more than that. It depends on what happens next spring. Some of the lawmen I've met can't leave well enough alone."

"It's the power, my friend. It goes to their heads."

Jim nodded in agreement, thinking all the time that power had already gone to the general's head.

Suddenly Patience spoke. "Joseph, I want to take Tommy back to Rawhide."

Kane glared at her. "Absolutely not. The boy must learn to be a soldier!" he snapped.

"But he can't take much more."

"Restrain yourself. I do what I want with you and my child!" The general's voice was ragged now and his cheeks flushed.

"Whoa!" Jim said, feeling his way carefully. "I don't hold with hurting women and children."

The general looked at Jim coldly. "This is a family matter. Besides, she's too easy on the boy."

"Women are like that," Jim said casually. "How old is the boy?"

Patience answered. "He's three."

Jim frowned. "That *is* a bit young. They don't even try to teach kids to read until they're five. Maybe you should send him back to town, General, until he's a little older."

He kept his tone bland, steadily eating his steak. But he waited tensely for the general's response.

"I've thought of that," Kane said after a moment. "But I want to keep him here. I will keep Patience here to care for him."

"Against her will?" Jim blurted unthinkingly. But the general didn't seem to notice the slip.

"Of course not. You'll see. Patience, you may go home tomorrow."

"Not without Tommy."

"You see, Jim? She stays willingly."

As much as he hated doing it, Jim nodded, as if he was satisfied.

One thing was clear. As Patience had said, the general was crazy, a madman, who had no business raising a child. If—no, *when* they got back to Rawhide, he would recommend Patience ask his cousin Nick to help her get legal guardianship of Tommy. The general couldn't possibly convince a judge he should keep the child.

As soon as the meal was finished, Patience

withdrew, rising without warning and leaving the tent, not waiting for the general's consent. She'd never been one to submit to someone else's control. Jim hoped the general could convince himself that she was being compliant. Otherwise, there was no telling what might happen to them all.

"PATIENCE," SHE HEARD someone whisper just outside her tent.

Lying awake next to Tommy, she quickly sat up and whispered in return, "Yes?"

"I'm going to slit the tent here in the back. Don't make any noise."

She turned to face the back of the tent. She saw a blade pierce the material. Then a hand parted the edges and Jim's face appeared.

"Oh, Jim! Thank you for coming."

"I'm sorry I didn't take you seriously when you called. I'm so sorry, Patience."

She blinked hard, hoping to disperse the tears. She'd needed him so badly she couldn't believe he was here. "Thank you."

"What the hell is Kane thinking, bringing a child up here?"

"I keep hoping he'll realize Tommy is too

young to be a soldier. He's very rough with him. I don't know what to do.''

"Tommy doesn't like him?''

"No!''

Jim shushed her, afraid they might be over-heard.

"Sorry,'' she whispered. "But the man is insane.''

"Yes, I can see that. Look, let's play this out as long as we can, but if it goes bad, we'll escape.''

"Do you think we can?''

"Sure. I'm going to get you out of here, one way or another, Patience, I promise you.''

"Jim, I... Be careful. I don't want you to get hurt.''

He grinned and her heart raced. She'd dreamed so long of his smile. It held everything she loved about him.

"I don't, either,'' Jim said cheerfully.

Then he extended his hand into the tent to stroke her cheek. "You take care of yourself and Tommy.''

"I will.''

Then he was gone.

Patience cupped her cheek, wanting the feel of his warm skin against hers to last. Could he do as he promised? Without getting hurt? She feared Kane would shoot him, or order him shot, if he discovered Jim had come to rescue her.

She did not want Jim Randall's blood on her hands.

Chapter Three

"Mommy!"

Patience came awake with a jolt. She stared at the little boy. "What? What is it?" she whispered.

"The general didn't come get me this morning. And they're making a lot of noise."

He was right. Patience could hear the sound of guns being fired. She was amazed they hadn't woken her. "Stay here," she said, and crawled the couple of feet to the tent opening and peeked out. Five men were lined up, their backs to their tent, firing at a target, a tin can, perched on a log about fifty yards away.

To her surprise, Jim was walking among the men, giving them tips on improving their aim. Kane was watching them, a satisfied look on his face. His lieutenants, who were always near him, didn't look happy. Maybe they were jealous of Jim, she thought.

Then she saw Roger approaching her tent, carrying a tray.

"Miz Anderson, I have some breakfast here for you and the boy," he said. "I have to clean up the breakfast things, and I'm afraid you won't get anything if you don't take this."

She immediately pushed the tent flap wide. "Thank you, Roger. You're very good to us."

He grinned shyly. "Yes, ma'am. If you'll give me your cups, I'll bring you some water, too."

She hurriedly handed him the tin cups she and Tommy had been given. "Thank you, Roger. Much appreciated."

"No problem, ma'am."

He returned in moments with the water, and Patience remained at the opening of the tent as Roger moved away, her gaze focused on Jim. He didn't exhibit any of the pompous authority Kane employed. He moved among those learning to shoot as a friendly helper, and it was obvious he was earning the respect of the men in a way Kane could never do.

As if her thoughts had conjured him up, she heard Kane's harsh voice. "Patience! You and the boy should be out of your tent. We have things to do.''

Patience's gaze swung to where Kane was standing a few yards away. He'd caught her staring at Jim. Not good.

''We're eating now,'' she replied. ''We'll be out after we've dressed.''

She withdrew from sight. Could she keep Tommy hidden from his father for the day? The boy wouldn't like being trapped in a tent all those hours. The storm had passed during the night, and he'd want out to run in the snow.

''Tommy, here's some breakfast. Some eggs and meat.''

''I don't like that. I want pancakes.''

Patience took her small son by the shoulders. ''Listen, Thomas. We're in danger. If we're ever to get back home to Grandma, we need to be strong. To be strong we've got to eat. There'll be time for pancakes when we're safely back home.'' She knew she sounded stern, but it was important the boy understand.

''Yes, ma'am,'' Tommy said softly, his head down.

''Roger brought us some toasted bread, too,'' she said encouragingly. ''It's probably cold by now, but it'll still taste good.''

They sat together, trying to stay warm, and ate silently. She took a swallow of the water Roger brought them and then offered the cup to Tommy. He didn't complain about not having milk to drink and dutifully took a few sips. Then they brushed their teeth with the water in the other cup and the toothbrush she'd brought from home.

"What do we do now?" Tommy asked.

"Well, I think you should get back under the covers. I have a new book for you to read. I have to go talk to Joseph, but you will be safer in here."

"A new book?" Tommy asked with excitement.

Patience was glad Tommy focused on the book. "Listen, baby, when I tell you to do something, I need you to do it at once. I can explain later, but...the bad man could hurt you if you don't do what I say."

Tommy nodded mutely.

She leaned over and kissed him. "Okay. Here's your book. Stay in here and read it until I come back."

Patience pulled on jeans and a sweatshirt over her long underwear. Then she added a big coat, actually her father's old sheepskin-lined leather coat, and gloves.

"I'll see you in a little while, Tommy."

When she emerged, the men were no longer target-shooting. Instead, the soldiers were donning all the outer clothes they had. She watched them, trying to figure out what was going on.

"Patience! Where's the boy?" Kane yelled. He was standing outside his tent.

"He's staying warm in the tent."

"Dammit! Get him dressed. We're taking a training hike."

"He wouldn't be able to keep up!" Patience was determined to keep her small nephew from going with the troops.

Jim stepped over to Kane and said something she couldn't hear.

"Never mind," Kane called after his consultation with Jim. "We'll train him later."

"Over my dead body," Patience muttered. She watched as the general called his men together. It appeared they were leaving behind four soldiers to prepare lunch, Roger among them. But Jim and all three lieutenants were being included in the hike.

Patience breathed a sigh of relief. In spite of her hatred for Kane, she knew she'd be safe from the soldiers he'd left behind because his men feared him too much to hurt her. Which made her wonder not for the first time why any of them followed him.

When the men filed out of camp, she wandered over to the big campfire. Roger and the other three soldiers were trying to figure out what to cook for lunch.

"But we gotta chop more firewood, too," one man said.

"I'll be glad to help cook while two of you chop wood," she offered.

"Oh, no, ma'am," Roger protested. "The general wouldn't like that."

"I don't think the general would care. And I'll tell him I insisted on it."

She organized the men and suggested they cook stew, which could be heated up whenever the men returned. After they chopped the meat and cut up what vegetables they had, Patience began mixing up the ingredients for biscuits.

"Ma'am, I can see you know how to cook," Roger said. "Too bad the general doesn't put you in charge of the meals."

"It's easy today, Roger. When we run out of vegetables, it won't be so good," she pointed out. "What does the general provide for your food when winter really takes hold?"

"I don't know, ma'am. We've only been here a couple of months."

Patience studied the man for a few minutes. "And do you agree with what the general wants to do?"

Roger looked puzzled. "What do you mean?"

"Why have you formed an army?"

"The general said we could be hired to protect people and make lots of money."

The three other soldiers nodded in agreement.

"I see. If you'll excuse me, I'll check on my boy."

She hurried back to her tent. Tommy was asleep, with his book on top of him. The past few days had taken a lot out of him.

When she thought the stew must be done, she returned to the campfire, filled two bowls and took them, along with some hot biscuits, to her tent. She gently roused Tommy to eat his hot meal. Then she allowed him to leave the tent so he could get some exercise.

With the general not around, life in camp was almost pleasant. Roger even indulged in a snowball fight with Tommy, letting him try to hit him with his little snowballs.

When Patience heard the others returning, she insisted Tommy go back with her to their tent.

After a while Roger called from outside, "Miz Anderson? I told the general about all your help and he was pleased."

"That was kind of you, Roger, but not necessary." She preferred that neither she, nor Tommy, be mentioned to the general. To her surprise, she didn't hear from the general the rest of the afternoon. She caught glimpses of him and Jim, but they seemed to be involved in either intense discussions or in training the troops. Judging by the grumbling of the men, she gathered they hadn't been trained until now.

She wasn't sure what Jim's purpose was, but he seemed quite happy to order the men about and keep them moving. He made no attempt to contact her. Even though that was best, she couldn't help being a little miffed.

How was he going to save them if he never spoke to her? Maybe she should've left this morning while they were out of the camp. She didn't think Roger or the other three cooks would stop her.

When Roger informed her she was invited to the general's tent for dinner, Patience asked him to feed Tommy again. She had no qualms about leaving Tommy with Roger.

The three lieutenants and Jim were again present for the meal. Good. She was anxious to see Jim again.

Kane greeted her with a big smile. "Good evening, Patience."

She immediately became more cautious. "Good evening," she muttered, not making eye contact with anyone.

"I understand I owe the delicious lunch to you," Kane continued.

She frowned and quickly looked up, wondering if the man was being sarcastic. She shrugged. "It gave me something to do." She paused, then decided now was as good a time as any. She would even placate him by using his title. "General, I need to return to Rawhide to care for my mother. I've been gone too long as it is."

There was a change of demeanor in the general. "I've said you can leave whenever you wish. I'm not holding you."

"But you know I can't go without Tommy."

"My son must remain here with me." His words were cold.

She fell silent and no one spoke again till halfway through the dinner. The general looked at her and said, "This meal isn't as good as our lunch. You make a much better cook than my men."

"Thank you," she muttered, not sure where he was going with this. She began to regret she'd made the stew. She would do well to keep to her tent tomorrow.

There was more silence.

When the meal was over, she rose to escape for the evening, but the general stopped her.

"Wait, my dear. I have made a decision."

She braced herself for what he might say.

"I think we shall marry."

She stared at him, completely taken aback.

"But, General," one of the lieutenants began. The general silenced him with a hand motion. "If you are to remain here, anyway, because of the boy, you must accept my protection. After all, you are an attractive woman. The men might think you were here for their, uh, entertainment. Instead of just mine."

Patience felt her cheeks flush, but she spoke clearly. "I am here for no one's entertainment. I am here for my son."

"Ah, but he's *my* son. Not yours. However,

with our marriage, I can give you more children.''

Patience stared at him. ''No! Never!''

''Mind your manners, my dear. You have no choice. Either you leave my camp or you marry me. Tomorrow would be the perfect day, don't you think, Jim?''

Patience looked at Jim for the first time. He hadn't shaved since he'd come to camp. He didn't look like her Jim. He met her gaze with a steady look. Then he said, ''As good as any other day, if you intend to keep her in camp.''

''You heard her. She refuses to leave. And it will be a long winter without a woman.''

''Your men will feel the same urges, General,'' Jim said, meeting Kane's gaze. ''If they see you enjoying such things, it will make their longing for female company more acute.''

''He's right, General,'' one of the lieutenants said. ''Send her and the boy back to town. They'll only cause problems.''

The general banged his hand on the makeshift table. ''I am the man in charge! As such, I deserve special benefits.'' He turned to Patience, still standing. ''Tomorrow, my dear, we will marry. And tomorrow night, you will warm my bed.'' He leered at her, and Patience couldn't hold back a shudder.

''You may go now,'' he said with a smile that made her ill.

JIM WATCHED HER leave the tent, his mind working furiously to come up with a plan to get them out of here safely.

One of the lieutenants said, ''General, you're making a mistake. The men will either leave or riot at your having a woman.''

Again the general slammed his hand on the table. ''Silence! I have made a decision. The woman might try to escape. Put double guards on her tent.''

''But you said she could go,'' Jim reminded him.

''Neither of them are going anywhere.''

''We could go into town, find some willing women,'' one of the lieutenants suggested.

Jim could tell the man was thinking of his own enjoyment, as well as his leader's.

''I will certainly let you go to town on occasion, but I need a woman close by. Patience chooses to remain with the boy. She will have to suffer the consequences. Plus, she'll help with the cooking. Quite an ideal arrangement,'' he said, smiling.

''Shall I do a guard rotation?'' Jim had tried to work his way into the general's favor by training the men today. It also served another purpose by tiring the men out so they'd sleep soundly.

''Not a bad idea,'' Kane said. ''Why don't you take the midnight-to-four shift?''

''Fine.'' That was perfect. He didn't bother to listen as the general assigned two of his other men. The third he gave the night off. They would each be supervising four men, double the usual two.

But Jim knew he had no choice about their departure. It had to be tonight. The general roused him from his thoughts with a question about the schedule for tomorrow's training.

The general loved the training they'd done that day. It made him feel powerful to have well-trained soldiers at his command. Of course, the men were not well-trained, Jim knew. In fact, they were rather weak and unskilled.

The general's encouragement came in the form of screams and threats. The men would soon rebel at such treatment. In Jim's opinion, this ''army'' had no chance to survive the winter. Inactivity or, worse, training at the general's hand, would discourage them. Finally, lack of entertainment, women and good food would push them over the edge. He still wondered how the general had held them together for so long.

"Your men were willing workers today, General. I commend you for motivating them so well. Do they all hold your political views?"

The general laughed. "No! I've told them we will be hired by people needing protection and we'll be highly paid. They think they're going to get rich."

"Do you pay them now?"

"Yes, with these."

He tossed a coin to Jim. Jim realized it matched the four he had with him. Frowning, he said, "I've never seen this kind of coin before."

"Of course you haven't. I had them made. I've told the men they will be able to exchange their coins for gold in the spring."

"What does the '30 p' stand for?"

The general laughed again. "It stands for the thirty pieces of silver Judas received for betraying his God. I was betrayed when God took my wife. Until he rewards me, he owes me. I use those coins to buy anything I want."

Steal, not buy, Jim thought.

"Unfortunately," the general went on, "the store owners don't seem to appreciate my coins. We have to spread our patronage around."

Jim nodded. "Will you be able to feed your men all winter?"

"Yes. I'm using my savings. It's not much, but enough to finance me for a year or two. By then, I will have gotten established."

Inwardly Jim marveled at the man's naive arrogance. He also doubted the "soldiers" intelligence for believing the man.

Jim brought the subject back to tomorrow's training, wanting to give the impression he intended to be there. He kept all thought of the escape out of his head—for the moment.

When they ended their discussion, Jim asked the first man on guard to wake him at midnight. Then he unrolled his bedroll and lay down. Now he had the time to plan their escape. He had to consider all the details because of the boy. And because the general would kill him if he caught them. Maybe Patience, too. And if he didn't kill the boy then, he would do so with his harsh treatment of him later.

With three lives at stake, he had to be prepared.

PATIENCE FOUND Roger still with Tommy when she got to the tent. "Thank you, Roger, for taking care of Tommy."

"I enjoyed myself." He paused and then asked, "Are you really going to take Tommy back home?"

"Why do you ask that?"

"That's what everyone is saying."

"I have to, Roger. Otherwise that madman will kill him. You do realize he's crazy, don't you?"

Roger looked uncertain.

"It's all right. You don't have to answer, but you should try to get away, Roger. You'll end up in jail or dead if you keep following him."

"But he killed the last man who tried to get away."

"Either wait till he's asleep and you have guard duty to run away, or do it when he next leaves camp. But do it."

"You're right. I will. I've been kind of drifting." Roger shook her hand and left the tent. Patience watched him go, hoping she hadn't made a mistake by being frank with him. But she hated the thought that gentle Roger could die at Kane's hands.

She hoped she and Tommy wouldn't die at

his hands, either. But they probably would if she didn't escape tonight. And Kane wanted her to marry him. She shuddered at the thought. Surely she could elude her guards tonight and get herself and Tommy away. Certainly Jim would realize they had to leave tonight. After all, he'd been present when she'd received her ''proposal.''

In preparation, she repacked their things, leaving anything not necessary to their safety. She'd brought her father's old coat because it was the warmest she owned. But also because it was big enough that she could button it up with Tommy inside.

She quietly worked while Tommy slept. But as the time drew closer to midnight, she despaired of Jim coming.

She crawled to the front of the tent and pushed back the flap only a couple of inches. The peaceful scene didn't please her. Then, just as she was about to withdraw, four men approached the area of her tent. Four? Kane had doubled the guard? Where would they station themselves? What was she to do now?

She watched again as the new guards poured themselves cups of coffee before taking their places. Suddenly she realized that one of the new guards was Jim. That explained why he hadn't contacted her. It would be safer for him to do so while he was playing guard.

She let the tent flap fall and reviewed her packing, wanting to be completely ready when he did come. Then she sat down, wrapping her arms around her knees and waited.

Chapter Four

Jim had decided to err on the side of caution. So he waited until 2:00 a.m., when the other guards would be less alert, and with any luck, have dozed off. Heart pounding, he made his way to Patience's tent.

His heart went into overdrive when he found the slit he'd made at the back of her tent had been lengthened and the tent empty. She'd already gone? She hadn't waited for him? Where was she?

Jim took a deep breath and gathered his thoughts. They couldn't have left without leaving tracks in the snow. Sure enough there was a single set—she was obviously carrying Tommy—leading away from the camp. How far had she gone?

She and the boy had made it half a mile from

the camp when he caught up with them. "Patience! Why didn't you wait for me?"

"Because you didn't come," she said.

"I wanted to be sure we could make it."

"*I* made it! You can go back and play soldier. You seem to be having so much fun!"

"When did you leave?" he asked.

"About one."

"You've only come this far in an hour? We've got to move faster." He looked around and said, pointing, "Sit on this log. We can't walk out of here."

"But I can't rest. I have to—"

"Just listen to me. I'll go back and get horses. But I have to be able to find you. So stay here." He waited until she nodded. "Promise me you will."

"I promise."

He found the camp, including the guards, asleep as he crept up to it. He circled the tents until he reached the rope corral. Quietly, he undid the rope. Then he moved silently among the horses until he found the two he'd brought with him. He'd chosen them because they were sure-footed and fast. As he led them out of the corral, several other horses followed, realizing they were free. He found his two saddles where he'd left them. He led the horses a few feet away from camp before he saddled them. Then he led them to the base of a big tree where he'd stowed some supplies.

Once he'd loaded all he could on the horses, he mounted one and checked his watch. Having to backtrack had cost him time. By the time he reached Patience and the boy again, it would be three o'clock. That gave them only an hour before the next shift of guards came on duty and the alarm would be raised.

But he knew better than to ride faster than a walk. He had to be sure he found Patience again. He picked up her trail, but soon he realized there was another set of adult-size footprints in the snow that occasionally appeared outside Patience's tracks—and they weren't his.

PATIENCE HAD DOZED OFF. Her first warning that she'd been discovered was a gruff voice ordering, "Stand up!"

She jerked awake, her arms encircling her child who lay sleeping against her stomach. As she struggled to her feet, she was afraid her shaking knees wouldn't hold her. She recognized her captor. It was Benton, the nastiest of the three lieutenants.

"What are you doing here?" Benton demanded, his rifle pointed at her.

"I...I had to go, uh, take care of business, and I got lost." Weak, but the best she could come up with.

"Likely story," he snarled. "Why do you have the boy with you?"

"Uh, he doesn't like to be left alone."

"Well, get up. I'm taking you both back to camp."

"I don't know how to get back, you see. That's why I haven't returned."

"Stupid woman. Follow your own tracks."

She wanted to say a lot of things to this jerk, but she restrained herself. She walked as slowly as she could, afraid to get too far away from where she told Jim she'd remain.

"Move faster," the man ordered.

"I can't. I'm exhausted," she said, leaning against a tree.

"Move it, or I'll shoot you and tell the general you were trying to escape."

She pushed away from the tree and kept moving, but not briskly, and she made as much noise as she could hoping Jim would hear.

Suddenly Jim was there, his rifle trained on the other man. "Get behind me, Patience," he ordered. To Benton he said, "Drop your rifle. I'm taking Patience and her boy home."

"You bastard! You were lying all the time!" He raised his rifle and shot, the bullet narrowly missing Jim's head. At the same time Jim squeezed the trigger and the bullet hit its mark. Benton fell to the ground, clutching his knee and Jim snatched up the man's rifle. There was no time now to think about the close call. "This way, Patience. Hurry!"

They reached the horses and he helped her and the boy into the saddle of one horse and mounted the other. "Stay right behind me. Can you manage the boy, or shall I take him?"

"I've got him."

Jim nodded and swung his horse around, changing directions, and led the way through the woods.

They pressed on for almost an hour before he felt sure they had a good lead. He hoped the gunshots had spooked the horses out of their corral and sent them scattering. He reined in his horse and waited for Patience to come up beside him.

She looked puzzled. "Why aren't we going down the mountain? I think we were even going up for a while."

"We didn't go down because that's where they'll assume we've gone. We're trying to avoid them."

"I know that!" she snapped. "I'm not dumb. But I wish you'd shared your plan with me."

"I haven't exactly had time. Even now, we can't rest for long."

"What if they find our tracks?"

"I expect they will—I don't imagine we've gotten away clean. All we've done is buy a little time. The general's pride has been hurt. He can't let you and Tommy, especially Tommy, get away."

She hesitated. Then all she said was, "Let's go on."

Without another word, he headed off and Patience followed. He'd wanted to assure Patience that he'd get her home safely. But he wasn't sure. They were still outnumbered and the escape hadn't gone as planned. He'd had to shoot a man, too. That would only add to Kane's fury.

If he could get Patience to the ranch, he could count on his family to provide for her safety. And she'd need the protection. The general wasn't likely to give up.

Another hour and the sun crept over the horizon. They had kept a steady, if not fast, pace.

He hoped they were putting a lot of distance between them and the general's men.

In spite of Patience's questions, he did have a definite destination in mind: the cabin his family used during the summer as a special trip for the kids. They'd find comfort there and maybe food. And he was very familiar with the trail that led down to the main ranch house.

But they had a few more hours to go.

He suddenly realized Patience wasn't behind him. He swung his horse around and trotted back to her.

"Why didn't you call me to stop?" he demanded.

"I thought I could handle things on my own." She had dismounted. Tommy was relieving himself not far away. "He had to go."

Jim drew a breath. "I understand, but we have to work as a team. Next time let me know, okay? How about you? Do you need to stop?"

"No."

"Come on, Tommy, let's go," he called softly. "I want you to ride with me." The little boy pulled up his pants and looked doubtfully at Jim. Then he looked at his mother. "Do I go with him, Mommy?"

"No, I can—"

"Patience, take a break," Jim said. "I can handle the boy."

"But I'm fine," she said. "You don't—"

"Let me do this for you, okay?" He summoned a smile. "It'll give Tommy and me a chance to get to know each other."

Patience gathered Tommy into her arms, gave him a kiss and whispered in his ear. Then she handed him to Jim.

The little boy reminded Jim of his cousin Toby's son. "Tommy, you're going to ride in front of me just the way you did with your mom. I want you to hold on to the saddle, all right? And if you get scared or need something, you can let me know. Okay?"

The boy nodded. Jim adjusted his wool cap to cover his ears. "Our horse's name is Jasper. Can you say that?"

"Jasper," Tommy said softly, and Jim kneed the horse into a walk. Tommy, believing the horse moved because he'd said his name, clapped with excitement.

Jim kept one arm around the little boy, the other on the reins. He was sure that Patience, despite her protests, must be exhausted. But when he looked over his shoulder, she was riding her horse just fine.

She was a remarkable woman.

Several hours later a small hand tugged on his arm. "What is it?" he asked, easing the pace.

"I'm sorry, Mr. Man, but I'm so hungry."

Jim slowed to a halt and slid out of the saddle then lifted Tommy down. "I think our horses are hungry, too."

"What's wrong?" Patience asked as she pulled her horse to a stop.

"Tommy's hungry, and the horses need a breather. Unfortunately I don't have anything for Tommy to eat."

"I do." She turned in the saddle and reached for a bag she'd added to the pack. She pulled out a candy bar. "Maybe this will keep you going for a while." She dismounted and handed it to Tommy.

Jim led both horses to a small area under a tree where the snow was sparse and the horses could find grass.

"Are you sure we can afford to take a break?" Patience asked.

"I think so, and if we want these horses to keep on going, we have to."

"Our pursuers will have to rest, too, right?"

"Not as much. We're making a trail for them."

"Oh." Patience looked at Tommy, who was happily eating his candy.

"It's going to be all right, Patience," Jim said, coming nearer. "I'm going to do my best to get you home safely. At least as far as the ranch. We'll figure out what to do next after we get there."

"Your family won't mind?"

Jim grinned. "You know my family. They always protect women and children." He put an arm around her.

She leaned against him, and it was a feeling he liked. "We're going to make it. I refuse to let a madman outthink me."

Their gazes met and held. Almost as if on cue, they both said, "I'm sorry—"

"You go first, Patience," Jim said.

"I...I wanted to apologize for our...last conversation." At his look of confusion, she clarified, "I mean our last conversation in Laramie. I had gone home for the weekend and I saw my sister and her husband. I tried to talk to Faith about Joseph, but she kept telling me he loved her. I knew he controlled her, but I wasn't sure it had anything to do with love. Anyway, I came back to school all fired up to make sure you weren't controlling me."

Jim frowned. "You thought I was controlling you?"

"No. At least, I knew what you wanted, but I was determined not to give in to you. Because of my sister. So I pushed you to make a commitment about our future."

Jim felt heat fill his cheeks. "You were right. But I was too young to... I wasn't prepared to settle down just then."

"It's all right. If I hadn't left school and come home, Tommy would've died along with Faith. I got there in time to get him to a doctor, which saved his life."

Jim looked at the little boy still contentedly munching his candy bar. "Thank God."

"Yes. He's the light of my life."

"Okay, now it's my turn to apologize," Jim said. "When I came home a couple of weeks later, I didn't call you. Instead, I asked my friends about you. Everyone told me you had a baby." He shook his head and then cleared his throat. "I figured you'd gotten involved with a man who had a child. I knew you'd gone on with your life without me. So I tried to put you out of my mind."

"I see."

"No, you don't, Patience. I never really put you out of my mind. I still care about you."

"I guess that's why you came after me."

"Yeah. Thanks for still caring enough to call me. I'm sorry it took me so long to come to help. I didn't want you hurt."

"Thank you. I'm not sure I deserved your concern, but I'm glad you came."

Suddenly he signaled her to be quiet and then stepped around her to peer into the forest. "Time for us to move."

Patience nervously looked over her shoulder. "Did you see something?"

"It's hard to tell." He retrieved the horses. He picked up Tommy and mounted his while Patience mounted hers. They set off again.

He encouraged Jasper to move quickly through the woods, where the snow wasn't as deep. They had one more slope to go down and another to climb before they got close to the cabin.

As Patience followed, she thought about what Jim had said. He still cared about her. Mild words, compared to the way she'd describe her feelings for him.

But first things first. She had to make sure she got Tommy home safely before she considered her own happiness. And if Jim had no interest in Tommy, she would have to let go of her dreams at last. Because Tommy was her responsibility and her life.

She forced her attention to her mount, because descending a steep hill was tricky. A fall would only complicate their escape.

When they began the climb, they slowed. There was a trail to follow, but it was narrow at times. Her fear of heights had her clutching the saddle horn. But she didn't dare close her eyes.

Once they got close to the top, the trail steepened even more. Jim stopped and dismounted, leaving Tommy in the saddle, clinging to the pummel. "Tommy, I'm going to lead Jasper, but I want you to hang on and stay up there. Can you do that? Can you hold on tight?"

"Yes," the boy said softly.

"If you start sliding, you call me."

"I don't know your name," the little boy said, his eyes wide.

"My name is Jim. Can you remember that?" Tommy nodded.

"Good." Jim turned to Patience. "You'll have to dismount, too. We've got to lead the horses over this part. Let me know if you get in trouble."

"Okay," Patience said, looking over her shoulder. "I haven't seen anyone on the down slope."

"Neither have I. Hopefully we'll be up and back in the forest before they get to that point."

"Yes. But Tommy…"

"He's going to hold on tight, right, Tommy?"

"His name is Jim, Mommy," Tommy told her, pleased with his new knowledge.

"Yes, sweetie, I know. Hold on tight."

They climbed in silence, saving their energy for the climb. Jim had warned her not to follow too closely in case Jasper got in trouble, and several times, the animal slid. Her heart leaped to her throat, as she feared for Tommy's safety. But her little boy held on bravely.

When Jim reached the top, he tied Jasper to a tree and lifted Tommy down. He set him on the ground nearby with instructions not to move until he was back. Then he hurried downhill to lead Patience's horse. She continued on up in front of him, grateful the climb was almost over. She checked on Tommy when she reached him. He seemed in good spirits. She was grateful he didn't fully understand what was happening.

"Okay, Patience," Jim said, "look through

the trees. Do you see that big rock sticking out?''

"Yes. Don't tell me we have to climb it!''

"No. I want you to take Tommy and ride toward that rock.''

"Without you?''

"Yeah, without me.''

He was standing there holding her reins. "Aren't you going to tell me why?'' she asked.

"I'm going to try to hide our tracks. Another attempt to buy us some time. I'll catch up with you.''

"When? And where? At the rock?''

"You're not actually going to the rock. You'll come upon a cabin. It's one my family uses in the summer. There should be food stored there we can eat. Beds we can sleep in tonight. It won't be long before it's dark. Then we can have a fire without worrying about the smoke being seen.''

"Can't we keep going?''

"It would be pretty dangerous on the trail at night. It's mostly switchbacks. One stumble and we'd go over the side. I don't dare try it in the dark. But we'll be off before daylight in the morning.''

"Are you sure?'' Patience asked softly.

"As sure as I can be. But if I don't show up…"

He stopped because she was shaking her head desperately. "Don't even suggest such a thing!"

"Patience, we have to face reality. I'm sure I'll get there before too long, but you have to be ready for anything. If I don't show up, there's a path leading to the east on the other side of the cabin. You follow it. When you start down on the switchback trail, get off the horse and lead him. Don't ride. There's a walkie-talkie in the saddlebag. You'll be in range by then. Call my home and tell them you need help. They'll come pick you up at the bottom of the trail and take you back to the ranch. Just tell them everything."

"Jim, I can't leave you!"

"You have no choice. You have to save Tommy, no matter what happens to me."

"I don't want you to be hurt. Jim, Kane will kill you! He's evil, as well as crazy."

"I know. But he'll have trouble catching me. Go on now. You're wasting time. Remember my instructions. And no fire until after dark. Okay?"

"Yes," she agreed, but she didn't move.

"Patience?"

Without a word she threw herself into his arms and kissed him on the mouth. It had been three years since they'd kissed, but it felt as if they'd never been separated.

Finally Jim put her away from him. "You're too much temptation, sweetheart. Go on, take care of Tommy. Tommy, be good for your mommy, okay?"

"I will, Mr. Jim."

He crossed to Patience, now mounted on her horse and handed her the reins to Jasper. Then he collected Tommy and set the child in front of her. "Don't unsaddle the horses. Just make sure they get water and feed. There's some stored in the cabin."

She nodded and avoided looking at him. He patted her hand, then stood back, watching as they rode away.

PATIENCE DISCOVERED that riding without Jim was scarier. His presence had meant safety to her. Now, not only did she have to comfort her son, she also had to reassure herself. She jumped at the least little sound, which she communicated to her horse, which grew more and more skittish.

"You're acting like a wimp!" she muttered to herself.

"What did you say, Mommy?"

"Nothing, sweetie. Are you doing all right?"

"Yes, but when is Mr. Jim coming?"

"Soon. He's walking, so it will take him longer."

"Why didn't he ride Jasper?"

"He has to walk because he's getting rid of our trail."

"Our tail? I don't have a tail, Mommy."

Patience sighed. She wanted to know when Jim would catch up with them, too. "I know you don't have a tail, Tommy. I said trail." She pulled her horse to a stop. Since she was leading Jasper, he stopped, too.

"Look behind us in the snow. Do you see where the horses walked? The mean man could follow us. Jim is brushing our tracks away."

"Oh. Will he be here soon?"

"Soon," she said, giving up explaining.

They rode on through the late afternoon. Then Patience saw movement through the trees. She stopped her mount at once and froze. Her horse, however, seemed a bit spooked about something.

Wolves, she thought. She knew there were wolves in the mountains. No doubt that was what had spooked her horse. She shivered. What should she do? She looked back at Jasper and discovered Jim had left his rifle on the saddle. Should she fire it, try to scare them away?

A rifle shot would be heard a long way away. It might even alarm Jim, causing him to not finish removing their tracks. No, she couldn't do that, no matter how much better it would make her feel.

What about when she got to the cabin? Would the horses be safe? She didn't know. How long would it take Jim to get there? Would *he* be safe from wolves? Should she go back for him?

No. You can't do that, she scolded herself. *Do what he told you.* But oh, how she wished he was there! Then she reminded herself that she'd been the head of the family for three years. But that was in Rawhide, a town she'd known all her life, and her mother was there, too. She'd never really been all on her own.

"Mommy!"

She pulled to a stop again. "Yes, Tommy?"

"I'm hungry again."

She dug into her coat pocket. "I have another candy bar for you, sweetie, but that's all until we get to the cabin."

"When will we get there?"

"Soon," she said, knowing that word would quickly lose any meaning for the little boy.

"We're going to Jim's cabin. He'll meet us there."

"I'm tired."

"I know you are, dear. But we have to keep going." If for no other reason than to keep the wolves at bay. She'd seen several pairs of yellow eyes in the darkening woods. The sun had already gone below the mountains and light was fading fast.

Like Tommy, she was tired. She hadn't slept at all last night. Adrenaline had kept her awake part of the time. Mind-numbing fear had done its share of the job, too.

She picked up the pace, though she felt mean doing so. The horses had worked hard. But she wasn't sure she'd last much longer. She checked again to be sure she could still see the rock. If she got offtrack, they might never find the cabin or their way home.

It was wonderful that Jim had put such faith in her. But she'd still rather have him with them. At least she would be able to light a fire once she got to the cabin. It was getting dark quickly.

But shouldn't they have reached the cabin by now? Had they missed it?

That thought almost paralyzed her with fear. Well, she thought, at least she didn't have to endure a snowstorm. She glanced up at the sky, noticing clouds covering the stars. Did that mean another storm was coming? Why hadn't she looked at the sky before?

Because she'd been too busy missing Jim and feeling sorry for herself.

Suddenly she caught sight of something from the corner of her eye. A cabin. Jim's cabin.

"Tommy, look!"

"Is that Jim's house, Mommy? Is he there?"

"Yes, it's Jim's house but he's not there right now. But we can go in and build a fire, get warm."

"Good, 'cause I'm cold and tired. And hungry."

She groaned. Her insides were hollow, too.

She reined in her horse in front of the cabin, where an old-fashioned hitching post stood. When she and Tommy were on their feet again, she tied the horses to the post, even though the poor animals were undoubtedly too tired to wander off.

She reached for Tommy's hand. "Come on. Let's go inside and start a fire. It's dark enough now. Then I'll put the horses in the corral."

When she tried the front door, it was locked. Locked? Jim didn't say anything about it being locked. She looked at the two windows that fronted the cabin. She tried to open them, but neither budged. There had to be a way in. She took several deep breaths. *Think.*

"Where's the key, Mommy?"

"I don't know, baby." She stared at the door as if she could will it to open.

"Maybe Jim hid the key like Grandma does."

"No, dear, I…what? What did you say?"

Tommy repeated himself.

Patience had pulled off one glove and was already feeling the ledge over the door. When her fingers came in contact with a metal object, she grasped it and sank to her knees. "Thank you, sweetie. What would I do without you!" She kissed her little boy's cheek. Then she inserted the key into the lock and opened the door.

"Mommy, it's cold in here, too."

"That's because we haven't built a fire." She discovered a wood box with kindling and enough logs to keep the fire burning for several hours. She'd have to look for a wood box outside, too.

With Tommy's eager help, she got the fire started in the old black stove, warning him not to touch the stove. "Now, while the fire makes things warmer in here, I'm going to go feed the horses. I want you to sit on this chair and not move while I'm gone.''

JIM WATCHED Patience and Tommy ride away, hoping he'd made the right decision. He didn't think Kane and his men could be too close, because if they'd gone down the mountain to look for them, as he thought, they'd have to retrace their steps back up before looking for their tracks. Then they'd have to spread out at least a mile from camp to find their tracks.

He figured the closest anyone would get tonight was across the canyon he and Patience had climbed out of. It would be crazy to try that at night.

He stared over at the next ridge. In the waning light, he could see nothing. He grabbed a fallen branch and began brushing away the tracks, as if they'd never climbed to the top of the ridge. Soon he moved into the woods, out of sight, which made him feel a lot better. His thoughts constantly flashed to Patience and Tommy. He felt sure she would find the cabin if she just headed toward that big rock. His dad had taught him that trick when he was a boy and afraid of getting lost.

Hiding their tracks was hard work, and he actually began to sweat. He sure had better be out of the cold once he stopped working. But for now the heat felt good.

He seemed to work for hours, thinking he'd never reach the cabin. It was pitch-dark now, with the clouds covering the moon. He wouldn't mind some snow during the night to perfect the job he was doing. Then again, he didn't want to be snowed in.

He wanted to get Patience and her son to safety. He'd done a lot of things on his own. But being responsible for the lives of others was something new. He would fight for Patience and Tommy with his last breath. He just hoped they got lucky and got away from that madman.

He caught the scent of a wood-burning fire. He must be nearly there, he thought.

He also caught a movement in the darkness. Wolves, he was certain. He pulled out his pistol, wishing he had his rifle with him. He began to work faster. When he reached the clearing for the cabin, he dropped the limb he'd been using and backed his way to the cabin.

He saw the horses in the corral. His dad and uncles had repaired the corral before they'd repaired the cabin. ''Got to take care of our animals first,'' his dad always said. They wouldn't get home tomorrow without their horses.

Patience had fed and watered them, he could see. He rubbed Jasper's nose affectionately and then climbed the porch. When he opened the door, Patience was standing near it, a narrow log in her hands.

''Building up the fire?'' he asked.

''No. If it wasn't you, I was going to hit whoever it was on the head.''

''I'm glad you recognized me,'' he said with a grin. Before he could say more, Patience put down the log and threw her arms around him.

''I'm so glad you're here!'' she exclaimed, burying her face in his neck.

''Easy, sweetheart,'' Jim soothed, holding her against him. ''Did you have any problems?''

She backed away slightly to meet his gaze.

''No...except you didn't mention the key.''

''I'm sorry. But it looks like you found it.''

''Well, actually Tommy did. He reminded me that my mother hides a key over the door outside.''

''Where is the little guy?''

''He fell asleep as soon as he ate.''

''You found enough food?''

"Yes. I've got it all ready for you. There's canned meat, beans and instant potatoes."

"I'm starving," he said. "That all sounds good. Glad to have running water and plenty of canned goods. Listen, you go ahead and get some sleep. You don't have to sit up and watch me eat. I know you're tired."

"I want to," she told him with a soft smile that made his stomach flip.

"Okay," he agreed, hoping his face didn't show how much he wanted her there.

He washed up in the spartan bathroom and came back to sit at the table. Patience had put out a plate of food. "This is great," he said with a grin, inviting her to relax. "Clearing our tracks took a lot of energy."

"Did you get them all erased?" she asked.

"Mostly. It would take a really sharp eye to see what's left." He took a bite of food, watching Patience. She was still tense. "Except for the lock, everything else went all right?"

"Well, I didn't know what to do about the wolves following us. Are the horses safe in the corral?"

"Yeah. The tin nailed to the lower rails keeps vermin out and the horses safe."

He took another bite. She *still* seemed tense. "And Tommy made it all right?" he asked.

"Sure. Except for asking every few minutes when Mr. Jim was going to come."

"I think maybe we'd better teach him to just call me Jim. I'm not used to the 'Mr.' part."

"I want him to show respect to adults."

"Yeah, that's a good thing, but I'd rather be his friend, Patience. Like I hope you consider me to be a friend." He reached a hand across the table and she took it. The warmth of her hand was such a contrast to the cold of the night, he never wanted to let go.

"Since you left university, have you...regretted not getting your degree?" he asked.

She shrugged. "I never had a major, you know. I'm not sure what I would've done after I graduated. It made me feel guilty. I mean, look at your cousin Caroline, going off to make the world a better place. Or your other cousin Tori, doing investments and accounting. They made their degrees count for something."

"You might have found your niche. A lot of kids don't declare a major until their junior year," Jim said, watching her.

"Maybe. When I got home after our..."

argument, I found Faith dying and her baby ready to enter the world. Kane walked out and Mom was in shock. Tommy needed me. Sitting in classes seemed unimportant compared to that.''

''I guess so.''

''Are you doing what you want to do?''

''Yeah. But I never expected to change my job because of school. Mom and Dad insisted on it. I'm raising my own herd. I'm breeding Charolais cattle. They're known for the weight they can carry.''

''Yes.''

''How are you and your mom making a living?''

''Dad had a good insurance policy. Tori invested it for us and we live on that. We can't spend wildly, but we make it.''

''Good. That gives you time with Tommy.''

''Yes.''

She pulled her hand free and began gathering up the dishes.

''Don't worry about doing the dishes, Patience. I can do them.''

''It won't take but a minute. We want to leave the cabin ready for the next person who needs it.'' With her back to him, she said, ''Do you think your family will mind coming to get us?''

''Of course not.''

''They might not approve of me.''

''Why wouldn't they? My mother thinks you're special.''

''We haven't told anyone about Faith's... I mean, everyone knows she's dead, but they don't know how it happened. She and Joseph left town right after they got married and didn't come back until she was ready to deliver. We didn't want to tell anyone about Tommy's father.''

''Wasn't my aunt Anna involved in saving the baby?''

''Yes. And Dr. Jon Wilson, too, Tori's husband.''

''And you think my mother wouldn't know?'' He laughed. ''Not that she ever spoke to me about you. Mom keeps her secrets.''

''She...she brought a present for Tommy after I brought him home with me.''

''I'm glad. I feel guilty that I wasn't there for you.''

''You hadn't made me any promises.''

''Oh, yeah, that's me. No-promises Jim.'' He

stood and moved to the counter beside her. "I was immature, Patience—and scared."

"Sometimes I'm scared, too," she said.

"Well, everything's going to be all right. And my family will be happy to pick us up once we're able to contact them. I promise."

"All right."

"Now, why don't you go up to the loft? It's fixed up real nice. I'll keep an eye on Tommy down here."

"He won't wake up. He sleeps like a log."

"Good. So will I," he assured her.

When she hesitated, he asked, "Is anything wrong? Other than the obvious."

"No. I'll…I'll go to the loft now."

She turned and slowly climbed the ladder.

Jim moved over to the bunk Tommy occupied. Curled up underneath the covers, the little boy looked very small. He couldn't imagine how Patience managed to grieve for her sister and take care of the baby at the same time. Yet Tommy showed no signs of his horrible beginning. Even the two days he spent with the general didn't appear to have done him any harm.

Jim certainly hoped not, anyway. He was a cute little boy. And smart.

With a sigh, he tugged the cover a little farther

up on Tommy's cheek. Hopefully tomorrow, he'd have him safe.

Moving to the sink, he put away the dishes she'd washed. Patience was a good woman. He'd done her wrong three years ago. He wished he'd been more understanding, been there when she needed him.

But maybe he could make up for it now. He could make sure she and her little boy got home safely.

He had just taken off his boots and begun unbuttoning his shirt when Patience called him. "Jim, would you come up here, please?"

Chapter Five

It seemed to Jim that he stood there staring at Patience from the bottom of the loft ladder for a long time. But it must've been only seconds. "Yes?" he asked.

"I...I'm scared. I can't go to sleep."

He climbed the rungs slowly, each step bringing him closer to something he'd dreamed about for the past three years—Patience holding open her arms to him.

He reached for her and wrapped his arms around her, saying, "You need to relax and get some sleep, sweetheart. Tomorrow is going to be tough, but we're going to make it."

"I can believe you when your arms are around me, but when I'm alone, I get scared. I know I should be more adult, but..." She dissolved into sobs.

Jim thought she'd held up very well, with no sleep, little food, intense cold and the threat of death hanging over her and her child. He rocked her against him. "Shh, honey, don't cry. Come on, let's lie down. I'll hold you for a while."

He pulled her down beside him on the bed. He'd already made sure he'd set the alarm on his watch so he'd get up early enough to get them on the trail by five. They would reach the switchback trail down in about an hour. If they got there before the sun came up, they could take a break then.

Bringing up the blankets to cover them both, Patience snuggled against him. Desire shot through Jim like lightning. He was too tired, though, and he couldn't betray the trust Patience had placed in him. It didn't take longer than two minutes of him holding her under the warm covers before her even breathing told him she was asleep.

He lay there another two or three minutes— at least that's what it felt like—when his alarm went off. He quickly turned the watch off and stared at it. It couldn't be four o'clock. He'd lain down with Patience at eight-thirty.

He realized he felt better. Not back to his usual strength, but better. He moved from Patience with reluctance. Her warmth had reassured him as much as his had her. The thought of crawling into bed with Patience for the rest of his life seemed as necessary as taking his next breath.

When they got home and had Tommy safe, they had a lot to talk about.

He climbed down the ladder and found Tommy still sleeping, looking as if he hadn't moved all night. After putting on his boots, Jim grabbed his coat and some feed for the horses. They got fed first.

The two horses were huddled together under the shed roof that extended over the corral. The smell of feed roused them. "Eat up, guys. You've got another long day before we get home."

He watched for a minute to be sure they were okay. Grabbing a nearby log, he broke the ice on the water trough so they could drink. Then he went back inside. Adding a couple of logs to the stove, with its glowing coals, upped the temperature level. They might as well start out warm.

Instant oatmeal didn't take long to fix. When he had three bowls ready and powdered milk in three glasses, he called to Patience.

"Patience! Breakfast is ready. You've got two minutes!"

Then he crossed to Tommy. "Little guy, it's time to get up and eat breakfast. Come on. I'll carry you to the bathroom, but you've got to hurry. It's your mom's turn next."

It took about ten minutes, but he soon had them eating their breakfast. He wished he'd found more food to take with them. All he had that would be easy to eat on the trail was beef jerky. Definitely an acquired taste, he admitted, hoping Patience and Tommy would eat it.

He poured Patience a cup of coffee to finish off breakfast.

"I want some, too!" Tommy cried, pushing his cup forward.

"Sure, Tommy."

Patience looked alarmed, but Jim poured several drops of coffee into the boy's milk, enough to give it a tan. "Try that, Tommy."

The little boy beamed at Jim. "I'm a big boy."

"Yes, you are. I know big boys who wouldn't have done as well as you."

The little boy drank his "coffee" with pride—and tried to hide his distaste for it.

"Okay, Tommy, one last visit to the bathroom and then we have to go."

When Tommy had left the table, Patience smiled at Jim. "Thank you for understanding. It made him feel so proud."

"He's done well, Patience."

"And…and thank you for comforting me last night. I shouldn't have fallen apart." She kept her gaze down.

Jim chuckled. "You comforted me, as well."

She turned bright red. "I'm glad."

"Take your turn with the facilities after Tommy. Then we'll be on our way."

"But it's still dark out there."

"We've got about an hour's ride before we reach the trail down. I'm timing it so we'll be there at sunrise."

Tommy came out and she disappeared into the bath. Jim, meanwhile, helped Tommy with his boots and coat. "Are you going to ride with your mommy today?" he asked.

Patience came out to answer that question. "Yes. He'll ride with me. He'll probably sleep a little more."

She slid into her big coat and pulled a wool cap over her blond hair, then put on her gloves. "I'm ready."

He took her outside, opened the corral and helped her mount her horse, then picked up Tommy and placed him in front of her. "Do you see where the trail starts off?" He pointed to the slight break in the trees to the east.

"Yes. Jim, don't make me go on without you."

He sighed. "Patience, I just want to backtrack a little bit to—"

"That will mess up all you've done to cover our trail. Come with us, please?" Her gray eyes pleaded with him.

After a moment he gave in. "Okay, I'll come with you. But if I tell you to go on without me, next time you have to go. I've put a .22 rifle on your saddle so you'll be able to protect yourself if something happens to me."

"Okay," she said.

Jim wasn't sure he trusted her to do as he asked. Now she knew how weak he was when it came to denying her.

He mounted Jasper and led the way to the trail. At first sight he'd put out the fire in the stove before he left the cabin, and there was no obvious sign that they'd been there.

His spirits were higher today. They were going to make it, he was sure. He'd done what he set out to do—rescue Patience and Tommy. And he'd made his peace with Patience, which was more than he'd hoped for.

And he intended to grow closer to her once they were home. He'd been an idiot to stay away from her for the past three years. Foolish pride had cost him a lot.

THE SNOW WAS crusty in places, which made it hard going that first hour. And because it was dark, Jim didn't want to push Patience and Tommy too hard.

In fact, the time just before dawn had a kind of dreamlike quality that lulled him into ignoring any noises. No one could've caught up with them that quickly.

A shot rang out.

"Ride on, Patience," he shouted as he pulled his rifle from his saddle and leaped to the ground, reins still in his hand. He found the nearest tree and began to search the forest behind him.

Shadowy movement drew a couple of shots from him. Then he waited to see what they would do next. He counted three men. That would be the general and his two lieutenants, he thought.

Jim was glad. He could hate those men—but not the innocents he'd spent a day training.

He risked a quick look behind him, expecting to see Patience riding quickly down the trail. She would reach the downward path soon and be out of range. Hopefully he could hold these three up until she was safe.

But he saw nothing. In fact, there were no tracks much farther down the trail from where he'd stopped. Patience couldn't have been hit by that bullet, could she? He would've noticed if she'd been shot. His heart almost stopped beating at that thought. He wanted to call out, to hear a satisfactory answer, but to do so would put her in danger.

Suddenly there was more gunfire. He swung around to face his attackers. He returned fire and knew he'd hit one of them. There was a scream and a body fell on to the snow from behind one of the trees.

That meant he only had two to deal with. The general wasn't the one who'd taken the bullet. If he had, his men would have turned back. They had no dispute with Jim or Patience. They hadn't wanted the boy in the camp in the first place.

More shots were fired, but Jim realized they were random, as if covering someone's tracks.

He swung around in time to face his attacker. One of the lieutenants had circled behind him and was lining up his shot. Jim tried to fire his rifle, but he heard a shot, and then another, and the man fell facedown in the snow.

Pain seared his right shoulder, confusing him. He thought maybe he'd gotten off a shot in spite of himself, but he didn't think so.

When he saw Patience step out from behind a tree with the .22 he'd given her from the cabin, he realized what had happened. She hadn't gone on, as he'd ordered. She'd gotten down from her horse to help him fight.

Ducking behind trees, she ran to his side. "Jim, you're shot!"

He loved hearing the anguish in her voice, feeling her soft hands on his face. More shots snapped him out of that dazed feeling. "Got to…return fire. Let them know we're still fighting."

Patience put her rifle barrel up against the tree to steady her aim and fired several shots.

Then she turned into a nurse, opening his jacket to look at the gunshot. In the meantime Jim heard the sound of a horse retreating. He caught a glimpse of a man on the horse, riding away from them.

"He's gone," Jim said, trying to sit up.

"Lie still. You're bleeding. Oh, Jim, I'm so sorry! I didn't want you to get hurt."

"I know. Look, it's not bad. I can still move my hand."

"Hush!" She took off her wool cap and used it as a pad to press on the wound and stem the bleeding. "Now I wish I'd paid more attention in my first-aid class in college."

"I don't think they were preparing you for— ouch—gunshot wounds."

"Probably not, but surely some of it would've helped."

"Where's Tommy?" Jim asked in alarm, trying to sit up until pain had him slumping again.

"I hid him and told him not to move until I got back."

"We've got to make sure he's safe."

"If you promise to lie still, I'll go get him and bring him here. Then I'll bandage your shoulder the best I can, and we'll start down the trail."

"Okay," he agreed.

With that she picked up her rifle and hurried in the direction from where she'd come. He was fortunate she hadn't obeyed him. He'd be dead by now. In moments she was bending over him again, Tommy at her side.

"You okay, little guy?"

"Yes. I took care of the horse."

"Good boy. You did better than me."

"Where's Jasper?" Tommy asked.

"He should be around. I left his reins dragging." All the horses on the Randall ranch were trained to stay put when their reins were left untied.

Tommy and Patience looked about. "I see him," Patience said. "If I get him, will you be able to mount with a little help?"

"Of course." He tried to sound strong and slightly offended at her question.

"Are you hurt?" Tommy asked, reaching over to pat Jim's shoulder. Unfortunately he patted the wound, which made Jim grimace.

"No, Tommy!" Patience called softly. She brought Jasper to a stop in front of Jim, then helped Jim sit up against a tree. She took her scarf off and put it inside his shirt.

"What are you doing?" he asked.

"I'm bandaging your arm with my scarf." She wrapped the long scarf around him, binding his arm, so it wouldn't move and cause him pain.

"Now, I want you to try to mount Jasper."

Since the wound was in his right shoulder, he could only use his left hand to pull himself awkwardly into the saddle.

"Good for you, Jim. I wasn't sure what we'd do if you couldn't get up there. Now, I'm going to put you on, Tommy." She settled the little boy in her saddle. "You think they all went away, don't you, Jim?"

"Yeah." He couldn't believe how weak he was. He barely had the energy to respond.

She swung up into the saddle behind her son, grasped Jasper's reins and headed down the path for the switchback trail that would take them to the Randall ranch. "If you feel faint, let me know."

"Right," he said, but the word came out slurred. What was happening here? He was supposed to be saving Patience, not the other way around.

Patience gave Jim a sharp look and pulled Jasper up alongside her mount. "Jim?"

"What?"

"Don't let go. Okay?"

"Yeah," he said.

It only took fifteen minutes to get to the downward trail. Patience was relieved to have reached it, but it meant that they had to go in single file. She remembered Jim telling her to lead the horses down.

She swung down from the saddle. "Tommy, I'm going to lead the horses. Can you hold on tight to the saddle?"

"Yes, Mommy." He sounded as if it was no challenge at all.

She tied her horse's reins to Jim's saddle horn. She took Jasper's reins and began the descent, keeping an anxious eye on both the riders. It was slow going. She had to stop after an hour for a breather. She also noticed Jim slumping lower and lower.

"Tommy, we're going to rest a minute. Do you want down?"

"Yes, Mommy, I need to pee."

"Yes, of course," she said with a sigh. They'd come across a wide spot on the trail, so she urged him ahead of the horses where he wouldn't get stepped on. Then she turned to Jim.

She was worried, but she didn't want to let him off the horse because she was afraid he wouldn't be able to get back on.

"Jim? How are you?"

He moaned, nothing more. She opened his saddlebags, looking for anything that would help her. She found a first-aid kit. She pulled her cap off his wound and replaced it with gauze. He was being jolted by the horse's movement, but it was the only way she had to get him down the trail.

She also found the walkie-talkie. Were they in radio range yet? Could she reach the ranch with it? They still had a long way to go, but it would help to know that someone would be waiting for them.

"I'm done, Mommy," Tommy announced.

She put her son back into the saddle and gave him a package of beef jerky, showing him how to take out one piece at a time.

"It's hard to bite," Tommy complained.

"That's why it's named jerky. You have to jerk on it." She gave a demonstration and then chewed as if she enjoyed it. Her son successfully followed her example.

She moved back to Jim's side. "Jim, how are you?"

"Thirsty," he muttered.

She felt his forehead and realized he was hot with fever. She found painkillers in the first-aid kit and gave him two pills and his canteen. He managed to get that down, which she found encouraging.

Then she tried to rouse someone with the walkie-talkie. "Hello, Randall Ranch? Can anyone hear me? Hello?"

She listened intently, but heard nothing. With a sigh, she put it back in the saddlebag. She'd try again later.

"Hello? Are you there?"

The disembodied voice scared her to death. Then she realized someone was answering her call. She grabbed the walkie-talkie and pressed the button. "Yes, we're here. We need help. Jim's been shot and he's not doing very well." She waited. Nothing. What was wrong?

She gave up again and moved toward Jasper when the voice came again. "Patience, you have to release the button when you finish talking so you can hear us."

"Oh, thank you. Did you hear me?" She released the button.

"Yes. Where is Jim shot?" The voice was feminine.

"In the right shoulder. I've bandaged it as well as I can, but it's still bleeding a little."

"Are you on the switchback trail?"

"Yes."

"We'll meet you with the ambulance."

Patience almost sobbed with relief. "Thank you."

She put the walkie-talkie back in the saddle-bag and started leading the horses down the trail again. They turned a bend and suddenly the entire valley was spread out before them. She was even able to pick out the Randall ranch. It had so many buildings it was like a small town.

It comforted her to know that someone down there was coming to help them. She looked back at Jim just in time to catch him as he slid out of the saddle. He was heavy and she staggered under his weight as she tried to get him back into the saddle.

"Jim! Jim, can you hear me?"

He moaned.

She stopped Jasper from moving. Then she managed to push Jim toward the wall of rock on the other side. She was going to have to be quick, she reminded herself. As he leaned on the rock, she slipped her foot in the stirrup and swung up behind him.

"Mommy, what are you doing?" Tommy asked.

"Trying to keep Jim in the saddle."

"Want him to ride with me? I'll share."

"I think we'd better do it this way. Now all you have to do, sweetie, is hold on."

She prayed Jasper could hold up under double weight. Some horses bucked when two people got on them. She gave thanks as she realized Jasper was well behaved. With a sigh, she locked her arms around Jim's broad chest and tried to hold the reins, too. But she realized she was at Jasper's mercy. Fortunately the horse seemed inclined to head for home.

So was she.

Chapter Six

Several hours of straining to hold up Jim's weight had numbed Patience's arms. At one point she heard voices. Thinking she was losing her mind, it was a relief to realize they were coming from the walkie-talkie in the saddlebag. She tried to reach it, but she almost lost Jim, so she gave up that idea.

His family was going to think she was very uncooperative, but she'd apologize later. After she got Jim down the mountain.

Tommy, who had held up remarkably well, had begun complaining again about being tired, even wanting a nap, and being hungry again. There was nothing she could do.

As they got lower, she caught sight of some riders moving toward them, but they were too far away and she couldn't identify them as friend or foe.

In fact, she was beginning to think everyone was her foe, and she'd never recover from the agonizing ride. When she heard hoofbeats and horses neighing, she thought she was imagining things. When Jasper patiently turned a corner on the trail, she was suddenly confronted with two riders.

Jasper came to a halt and threw his head up. Patience held on for dear life, afraid the horse was going to finally give her trouble.

The first man dismounted and came toward her and she realized it was Toby Randall.

"Oh, Toby, I didn't recognize you for a minute," Patience said with a gasp, sagging momentarily, which caused Jim to shift.

Toby hurriedly reached for Jim, giving Patience some assistance.

"I'm sorry. He's heavy," Patience said.

"Well, I guess. We wondered why you didn't answer the walkie-talkie, but I reckon I understand. You couldn't let go of Jim."

"Mommy wouldn't even hold me," Tommy added, wanting some sympathy, too.

"How about Drew and I help with Jim? That will free your mom to see about you," Toby soothed. He turned to Patience. "We've got a carrier rigged up to fit between the horses. We'll put Jim on that.''

''But the trail's not wide enough,'' she said in concern.

''I know. We'll show you.'' He motioned to Drew, who had some long poles tied to his saddle.

Drew jumped down from his horse and walked to Patience's side. ''How's old Jasper holding up?''

''He's been wonderful, never complaining.''

''Yeah, he's one of Jim's favorites.'' As he talked, his eyes were examining his brother. ''Has he come to?''

''Occasionally, but he's running a fever and still bleeding a little. I'm so sorry he got hurt. I never wanted…'' She was on the verge of tears as she made her apology, but both men waved her words away.

''We know that, Patience. And you're bringing him home. Aunt Megan will be thanking you for a long time.''

''We've been worried about Jim since he left,'' Drew said. ''I should've volunteered to go with him, but when he told me he was leaving I was still half-asleep. I'm not too bright until about 10 a.m.,'' he added, his cheeks turning red.

Patience smiled slightly, too exhausted to talk anymore.

''I'll go put my horse in the lead position and put the carrier on his back. Drew's horse will get the other end of the carrier. Then we'll transfer Jim to it,'' Toby explained.

Patience and Tommy watched the two men get ready to transport Jim.

As soon as the stretcher was ready, both men eased Jim off the horse and carried him to the stretcher, putting his feet at the front so his head would be on the high end as they went down the mountain.

Patience rubbed her arms to restore circulation. When she finally bent them, she cried out in pain.

''You okay?'' Toby asked.

''My arms are a little stiff,'' she explained, embarrassed.

''Mine would be, too.'' Toby's gaze moved to Tommy. ''Say, Tommy, since your mom needs to rest, why don't you ride with me for a while? We'll beat your mom to the bottom if you ride with me.''

Her normally shy little boy took the bait and agreed at once. "I like to be first," he declared.

Toby crossed to Tommy's horse and held out his hands. Tommy reached for him, delighted to be out of the saddle.

"I think it's my nap time, 'cause I almost fell off my horse."

Toby grinned. "You can go to sleep on my shoulder if you want."

"Okay."

"Toby," Patience said, "Jasper has taken the brunt of the weight. Should I transfer to the other horse?" she asked.

Toby looked at Jasper. "No, I think he'll be okay. It's only about an hour's ride away. They can get the vehicles close these days."

Before she could speak again, Jim roused and she heard him mutter, "Patience? Tommy?"

Drew answered. "They're here. They're safe, bro. You did it. You got them back."

Jim closed his eyes and sighed. "Thank God."

The rest of the ride was completed in just under an hour. When they got close enough to see a SUV and a truck with a horse trailer attached parked at the bottom of the trail, Patience knew their ordeal was about over.

She was so grateful that the two men had come up to meet them because she wasn't sure she could've made it this far supporting Jim in the saddle and taking care of Tommy.

She recognized Jim's mother Megan and his aunt Anna as they rushed up the trail on foot to Jim's side. Anna immediately began checking his pulse and the status of the wound. Megan leaned over his other side, held his hand and talked to him.

Patience was too far away to even know if Jim responded to his mother. She was amazed to feel envy when it should've been a relief to be rid of the responsibility. But *she* wanted to be the one who made him well, who spoke to him, who roused him from his misery. Patience shook her head. Obviously she was over-wrought.

By the time she got to the bottom of the trail, they already had Jim transferred to the SUV. She dismounted. Fortunately she kept hold of the saddle horn. That was all that kept her from sprawling on the grass, facedown. Both her arms and legs were shaking.

Suddenly arms were around her.

Megan told her to lean against her. "I owe

you so much for bringing Jim home,'' she said as she walked her to the SUV.

''Oh, no, Mrs. Randall. I owe Jim. I would never have gotten away without him. I'm so sorry he got hurt.'' The tears began flowing this time. She couldn't stop them, adding to her embarrassment. ''I'm so sorry. I never cry,'' she told Megan between sobs.

Suddenly, Anna was by her other side. ''Patience, Toby will take Tommy to the ranch. You will ride with us to the clinic. You need to be checked over after that ordeal.''

Then Patience was in the back seat of the SUV with Megan beside her and Anna up front driving. Jim was resting comfortably in the third back seat. Toby and Drew were getting the horses together to take them back to the ranch, along with Tommy. Patience closed her eyes and dozed.

''DO YOU THINK Jim will be all right?'' Megan asked Anna softly.

Anna looked in the rearview mirror. ''Megan, he's going to be fine. It looks like the bullet didn't hit anything major. He's lost more blood than I would've liked but Patience got him down the mountain the best she could. That wasn't easy.''

''I know. Both she and Tommy deserve a reward.''

Anna smiled. ''We've got *our* reward, getting Jim back. He'll be up and around in no time.''

Megan sighed. ''You know, Anna, I just want all my kids to be safe and happy. That's all.''

''I know. I used to worry about Tori, but now that she's settled with Jon and they have their baby, I don't worry as much. Now Jessica, that's another situation.''

''Yes. Elizabeth's marriage to Toby is wonderful. We know him so well. But I've still got two to settle down.''

''I think we're all spoiled. We all have such good kids.''

''We do. We really do.''

Anna hit the paved county road and increased their speed. In a few minutes they'd reached the clinic in Rawhide. An exhausted Patience had fallen asleep. Jon Wilson, the only doctor in Rawhide and Anna's son-in-law, had been watching for them. He met the SUV as Anna cut the engine, helping the one orderly they had move Jim onto the gurney to wheel him into the clinic.

"How's he look, Anna?" Jon asked.

"He'll need transfusions, hydration, antibiotics. I'll let you take over the rest. And we want to admit Patience, too. She'd needs hydration, food and some rest."

Since Jon had been there when Patience's sister died and Tommy was born, he knew Patience. "Where's Tommy?"

"Toby is taking him to the ranch. He and Davy can play together. Elizabeth will look after him. He'll be fine. Oh, and his grandmother is staying with us, of course."

Jon looked at Megan. "You have Mrs. Anderson at the ranch? I hadn't heard that."

"I looked in on her after Jim left. She was so shaken by Tommy's being taken and Patience looking for him that I helped her pack and took her home with me," Megan explained.

"You're a good woman, Megan," Jon said.

He'd sent the orderly in to bring another gurney for Patience. "Looks like the past few days have been hard on her," he commented softly.

"Yes," Anna agreed. "That's why I thought we should bring her in, too. She supported Jim's weight on the horse for a number of hours."

Jon reached into the SUV to pull Patience from Megan's arms and then lift her onto the gurney. "Well, looks like I'll be busy for a while. By the way, have you contacted Chad?"

"No, Jon. Since the men left to look for Jim, they've pretty much been out of radio range," Megan said. "I wish he was here. But Anna says Jim will be all right."

"I'd never bet against Anna," Jon said with a smile. He began wheeling Patience toward the hospital door. As soon as he got in, he ordered an IV for her and treatment for Jim. Within an hour, Patience was fully awake and seemed surprised to find herself in a hospital bed.

"Tommy! Where is he?" she asked, pushing herself up to a sitting position. She was surprised at how hard that simple movement seemed to be.

Megan, who was still at the hospital keeping an eye on both Jim and Patience, suggested they call the ranch. When Red answered the phone, she asked to speak to Elizabeth. She explained that Patience was concerned about Tommy. She then handed the phone to Patience.

"Oh, Patience, we're so glad you got Jim home," Elizabeth said. "And Tommy is doing just fine. Red fixed an early supper for him and he ate a big meal. Then he played with Davy for a while. They get along so well. Now he's asleep in Davy's room."

"Thank you, Elizabeth. I really appreciate what you've done." Patience was finding it difficult to swallow.

"Your mother spent some time with him, too. She hopes to see you tomorrow. I promised to take her in the morning to visit you."

"Thank you," Patience said again.

"Patience, you saved my brother. I owe you so much."

Patience, tears falling again, held out the phone for Megan. "I can't seem to stop crying," she gulped.

"Darling, what are you crying about?" Megan asked after a brief conversation with her daughter.

"People keep saying I saved Jim, but he saved me and Tommy. We're the ones who are in his debt. I never would've gotten away from Kane without Jim. He risked his life for us."

Megan wrapped her arms around her. "Things will be better tomorrow. Jim will be much better and so will you. They're bringing you some dinner now," Megan said just as the nurse arrived with a tray. "I'm going to make sure you eat it all."

"Why aren't you with Jim?" Patience asked.

"He's not conscious yet. Anna is with him.

She can help him more than I can, and she promised to let me know when he wakes up. But they don't expect that until tomorrow at the earliest.'' Megan smiled. "I wanted you to have someone with you, too.''

"Thank you," Patience said.

Patience gave the meal a good try, but after a while, she couldn't eat anymore. Soon her eyelids grew heavy.

Megan sat by quietly and watched her fall asleep.

Wearily Megan got to her feet and walked down the other hall to Jim's room. Pushing open the door, she found Anna sitting by Jim's side.

"He hasn't come to yet," Anna told her, "but his fever has dropped, and he's resting more comfortably. The bullet is still in his shoulder. Jon is going to operate in the morning.''

"Will Jim be all right?"

Anna nodded. "I'm sure he'll be fine. But I'm going to scrub for the surgery.''

"Oh, Anna, I know you're tired already, but it will make me feel so much better to know you and Jon are taking care of him." Megan wiped away a stray tear that escaped. "Now I'm feeling like poor Patience.''

"Don't worry. It's a normal reaction to the stress you've been under."

"Mom?" Jim said faintly, grabbing both women's attention. He was awake.

"Jim!" Megan exclaimed, reaching out to touch her son.

"Where're Patience and Tommy?" he asked hoarsely.

"They're fine. Patience is spending the night here, but she'll go home tomorrow. Tommy and his grandmother are at the ranch."

"Keep them there," Jim said. "Please."

"Well, of course they're welcome to stay, but why—"

"Keep them there," Jim said again as his eyes closed.

Anna checked his pulse and the IV. "He's drifted off again," she murmured. Then she looked at Megan. "Why do you think he wants them to stay at the ranch? So he can see Patience?"

"No. I think he's worried about their safety. Until he's better able to talk, we're going to do what he wants." Megan frowned as she watched her son.

"I'm going to sleep here tonight," Anna said. "That way I won't have to get up early and drive in. We've got another front coming in soon. You'd better get started for the ranch.''

"I'm not going home. I'll call Elizabeth and tell her. With our husbands out of touch, still looking for Jim, no one else will dare fuss at me," Megan told her with a smile. "I'm going to be here for Jim's surgery."

Anna nodded, clearly not surprised by Megan's decision. "How about we share a room, then?"

"Sounds good," Megan said, reaching for the phone.

Chapter Seven

When Patience awoke the next morning, a terrible sadness seemed to hang over her.

When she turned her head, she saw Megan dozing in a chair beside her bed. She wasn't sure why Jim's mother was still beside her.

Patience decided to try to make it to the bathroom without waking Megan, but when she stood, she realized she was woozy. A quick grab for the bed saved her, but the commotion disturbed Megan.

"Patience? What's wrong?" Megan sat up, a startled look on her face.

"I'm sorry. I needed to go to the bathroom, but the room began to spin." Patience felt tears gathering in her eyes. Ridiculous. Why was she crying?

Megan reached over and pressed the button to

summon the nurse. "I'm not sure they want you walking around."

"But I'm not sick."

"No, but they gave you a sedative early this morning, and its effects may not have gone away yet. Don't you remember waking up and telling us about your nightmare?"

Before Patience could tell her that she did not remember, the nurse entered the room and Megan asked her to help Patience to the bathroom. After the nurse helped her back to bed, minutes later, she announced, "Breakfast trays just arrived. I'll bring both of you some breakfast."

"I'm not hungry," Patience said.

"If you want to go home today, you better eat a good breakfast." With a brisk nod the nurse left the room.

Patience frowned, then said, "She didn't give me much choice, did she?"

Megan chuckled. "No. Are you feeling better this morning? More rested?"

"Yes. Yes, I am. And I'm going to eat so I can go home. And Mom and Tommy will come with me, so we'll all be out of your hair, Mrs. Randall."

"Call me Megan. You know, there are a lot

of Mrs. Randalls. Even Elizabeth is Mrs. Rand-all.'' Megan smiled warmly.

Patience smiled back and nodded, not mentioning how she'd once thought she would also be a Mrs. Randall.

The breakfast trays arrived and they both ate in silence. Patience discovered she had an appetite, after all.

At last she asked, ''How's Jim this morning?''

''We should know soon. He's in surgery—they're removing the bullet. We should know any time now.''

There was a knock on the door and Anna entered. ''The operation's over and Jim came through just fine. Jon got the bullet out and the wound is clean. He should be going home in two or three days.''

Megan sighed with relief, but Patience stared at Anna in horror. ''The bullet was still inside him? I never thought of that. He must have suffered terribly on the ride down the mountain.''

Anna came over and patted her hand. ''Nonsense. I'm sure it would've hurt just as much if the shot had gone right through. He probably would've bled more, too. You did everything you could.''

"It's all my fault," Patience said, her voice trembling. "He'll never forgive me."

Megan cleared her throat. "I'm quite sure you're wrong, dear. Jim's conscious thoughts were of you and Tommy. He wants you both to stay at the ranch until he's recovered. You will, won't you?" Shamelessly she added, "It will make Jim rest easier." She figured Patience's feelings of guilt, however misplaced, would force her to do what Jim wanted.

She was right. "I...I suppose we could stay."

"It's a good idea, for Jim's sake. He won't worry if you're with his family." Anna gave her a big smile. "And we'll love having you."

"Elizabeth said Davy is delighted to have Tommy there to play with. His little sister isn't that much fun, according to him." Megan shook her head in mock dismay. "Does Tommy wish he had a brother or sister to play with?"

Patience blushed. "Sometimes he asks if he can have a brother. When he goes to Sunday school and plays with the other children."

Megan smiled in sympathy. "Kids never understand."

Patience nodded, not wanting to discuss the problem of having a child with no man in her life. But after her disgust with Joseph's treatment of her sister, her argument with Jim, and then her sister's death, Patience didn't want to discuss anything having to do with her love life.

"Can we see Jim?" Patience asked, anxious to change the subject.

"He's in recovery. In a couple of hours, just before lunch, we'll have him in a room. Of course, you'll be more comfortable with a robe, since all you're wearing is a hospital gown that ties up the back."

Patience blushed again. "I don't have anything of my own here," she said, disappointment in her voice as if she thought she wouldn't be able to see Jim.

"We'll get you a robe," Megan assured her.

"Oh, Megan, thank you. I...I would like to see Jim."

"I think he'll like seeing you, too." Megan smiled. She was feeling much better to know that her son was out of surgery and doing well. "Now, if Chad would just get home, I'd be a happy camper."

Patience sent her an apprehensive look.

Megan noticed and said, "Oh, dear. I suppose you wouldn't have known. My husband, Chad, and several of the Randall men went out to find

Jim. We haven't been able to contact them to let them know you've all been found.''

CHAD RANDALL had taken off after his son the day following Jim's departure. He'd gathered together his cousins and three brothers, and gone to the sheriff, demanding they look for Jim and Patience. After two days, they'd had little luck in finding any substantial trail and were heading back home.

"Hey! Look at that smoke," Brett Randall said. He gestured at the black plume of smoke ahead of them.

After a few minutes Chad said, "It doesn't appear to be moving. Don't think it's a forest fire.''

"Maybe the snow's slowing it down," Brett returned. "Clouds are piling up—could be another storm soon. Maybe that'll take care of the fire.''

"Maybe," Jake said, as he scanned the skies. "I'd hoped we'd make it to the cabin tonight, but I don't think we can. We've only got a couple of more hours of daylight.''

When the sun sank behind the mountains, they camped across the canyon, leaving the crossing until morning. They'd already noted that the smoke had lessened, almost disappeared, in fact, and assumed the snow already on the ground had curbed it.

There was no conversation around the camp-fire that night. They were all tired and more than a little worried. They knew Jim and Patience had come this way, but they had no idea where they were or even if they were alive.

As soon as daylight arrived, the men began the descent and then the climb to the other side. When they got to the edge of the clearing, they came to an abrupt halt. All that was left of the cabin was charred remains. The smoke they'd seen yesterday had been the cabin burning.

The Randalls were stunned. Jake dismounted and moved closer to the remains. After studying them for a moment he said, ''Someone set this fire.''

''Could've been lightning,'' Chad suggested weakly. He thought of the times they'd spent here with their wives and children.

''In a snowstorm? No. I smell kerosene— probably that fire starter we brought up here a couple of years ago. There was still half a can of it left.''

Several others got off their horses to help Jake search the remains. Chad stayed mounted, frozen with fear. Had Jim been in the cabin when it was torched?

"No bodies," Jake finally said.

Chad almost fell off the horse in relief. "You're sure?"

"Yeah, I'm sure," Jake said. "You okay?"

"As good as I can be, not knowing where they are."

"We're gonna find them," Pete assured his brother.

Suddenly Brett pointed to the sky. Everyone stared at the buzzards circling in the distance.

"We're wasting time," Chad finally ground out. "There's nothing we can do about this now." He gestured at the charred remains.

"You're right," Jake growled. "Let's go. Where those buzzards are circling looks to be on the way home. We should make it there tonight."

The men remounted and rode toward the trail that would take them back to the Randall ranch. They'd almost reached the trail when the buzzards they'd seen suddenly flew up in front of them.

Jake swung down from his saddle. "It's a dead body."

Chad's heart squeezed in pain. "Jim?" His voice was hoarse.

"Nope. I don't recognize him, but he's pretty messed up from the birds."

Chad had to look at the body, just to be sure it wasn't his son. Then he glanced up and noted another flock of buzzards circling not far away. He pointed. "Look."

He began walking in that direction and Pete joined him, his hand on his brother's shoulder. "This one won't be Jim either, brother. I'm sure he's okay."

"I have to know," Chad muttered. Again, what was left of the body clearly wasn't Jim. Chad felt tears in his eyes at the relief. Did this mean his son had survived? That he had killed the men?

"We can't identify the bodies, Sheriff," Chad said. "Maybe they were with some paramilitary group."

"I'll talk to Jim, but I'm sure the shooting was in self-defense, Chad. Don't worry."

"I'll stop worrying when I see my boy alive and well," Chad replied, turning away to hide his fears.

Since they didn't have extra horses to carry the bodies back to town, they dug two shallow graves to keep the bodies away from the buzzards and other vermin. The sheriff would return with the Coroner to take the men's remains back to be identified. The work took several hours out of the Randalls' day.

"Looks like we'd best make camp. We'd be fools to risk going down the switchback in the dark." Jake sighed and looked at his family for agreement.

"What about the storm?" Chad asked. "It looks like it's going to dump a lot of snow."

"We'll start early and maybe miss the worst of it. Down low it won't be as bad. We can use the walkie-talkie after we get partway. Find out if there's been any word on Jim."

Chad shrugged and unsaddled his horse. They had ridden on to the start of the trail, getting away from the bodies they'd buried. There wasn't much cover, only a couple of large boulders. They all laid out their bedrolls at the base of the boulders.

About four in the morning Chad woke up to find himself covered in snow. He knew it would take them a long time to get home in this weather.

After trying to find some dry wood to add to

the fire he looked up to discover Jake standing over him.

Jake whispered, "I covered some wood with a tarp yesterday evening. It's dry. I'll get it."

Leave it to Jake to think of that, Chad thought. Jake had been father, as well as brother, to Chad for most of his life. He always knew he could rely on Jake.

Soon they had the fire burning steadily. Jake put on the coffeepot. "I reckon we'd better get home today. This is the last of our coffee," Jake said.

"There's not much to eat, either," Chad remarked. "Just beef jerky. Makes me think fondly of Red's breakfasts."

"Don't mention that," Jake warned. "It makes me even hungrier."

Their cousin Griff asked groggily from his bedroll, "Time to get up?"

"Naw," Jake responded. "You can sleep another hour if you want."

Griff shoved back his sleeping bag. "With you two yakking, I guess I might as well join you."

"Bring your cup. Coffee's about ready."

The three of them sat huddled around the fire and passed the time with remembrances. Chad kept checking his watch. Jake and Griff noticed, but then they'd come up with another story that brought a smile even to Chad.

By six, everyone was awake, having coffee and eating strips of beef jerky. It was still snowing, but not as furiously as it had been earlier.

"Can we get down the trail?" Chad finally asked, knowing his judgment was shot to hell. He just wanted to find out about Jim.

"I don't think we can ride down, but we can walk it. About halfway, we should be able to rouse someone at the ranch and get a ride once we get to the bottom."

"Then let's go," Chad said.

"Okay, brother. Lead the way."

They began their descent, moving slowly through the snow. Fortunately the snow hadn't completely covered the trail. They had no trouble following it.

Around eleven, Jake halted the procession. He pulled out a walkie-talkie and called the ranch. His wife, B.J., immediately answered. "Jake? Where are you? Are you all right?"

"I'm fine, sweetheart, we all are," Jake assured her. "Have you heard from Jim?"

"He's in the hospital. He was shot, but they

operated early this morning to get the bullet out and he's doing fine.''

Chad dropped his horse reins, moved over to Jake and reached for the walkie-talkie. ''What happened?''

''We don't know for sure. But Patience got him down the mountain and he's in good hands.''

''And the little boy?'' Chad asked.

''He's fine. He's staying with us.''

''Where's Megan?'' Chad wanted to hear his wife's reassurance.

''She's at the hospital, Chad. She's with Jim and Patience.''

Jake took back the walkie-talkie. ''We'll be down in about four more hours, we hope. Can you pick us up?''

''Sure. Hurry home.''

Chapter Eight

Megan found Patience a robe and they began to make their way to Jim's room.

A nurse came running after them. "Mrs. Randall? You have a phone call. They said it was important."

Megan didn't hesitate. "Go on to Jim's room, Patience. I'll be there in a minute."

Patience wasn't sure she could face Jim alone. She owed him so much and there was no way to repay him.

She stepped to the door of his room. He'd just been brought in from the recovery room and a nurse was settling him in, arranging his pillow and checking his stats.

"May I come in?" Patience asked.

Jim turned his head and saw her. "Come in," he managed.

Patience looked at the nurse, who nodded. "If you sit in that chair over there, he'll be able to see you without straining himself."

Patience went to the chair she indicated.

"Sit down," Jim said, his voice slightly slurred. "Are you okay?"

"Of course I am. You're the one we're all worried about."

"I don't remember much after I was shot," he told her.

"No. You were running a fever. I didn't even check to see if the bullet had come out. I didn't know what to do but try to get you down the mountain."

"I'm glad you did. How's Tommy?"

"He's fine. I talked to him this morning. He's enjoying playing with Davy." Her son had scarcely had time to waste on the phone. Patience was glad he was happy, but she was also a little hurt that he hadn't even missed her. "It's amazing how quickly kids recover."

"Yes, it is." There was an awkward pause before Jim asked, "Where are Mom and Dad?"

"Your mother had a phone call. And your father—"

"Will be home tonight," Megan said as she came through the door. "That was B.J. calling.

Jake called her on the walkie-talkie. She's going to pick them up in a few hours.''

"Dad was still in Cheyenne?" Jim asked, clearly puzzled.

Patience looked at Megan, saying nothing.

"Uh, dear, your father was worried about you going off on your own to face those men...and he decided to go after you in case you needed backup."

"And Uncle Jake went with him?"

"Well, yes, and, uh, the others." Megan busied herself smoothing the wrinkles on his covers.

"What others?"

"All your uncles, including Griff, and the sheriff."

"Damn! Do they think I'm incompetent?"

Before Megan could reply, Patience said, "No, they just love you. You should be grateful that your family loves you like they do." After a moment of silence, she stammered, "I...I'm sorry. I shouldn't have said—"

"It's okay, Patience, you're right. But it's hard to live up to the Randall standards," Jim told her, then asked his mother, "Did they run into trouble with Kane's 'army'?"

"I don't know. B.J. said they're all okay, and

they'll be home tonight." Megan relaxed, showing again how relieved she was.

"Okay," Jim said. "When do I get out of here?"

"I assume in a couple of days. I know Anna was concerned because you lost so much blood," Megan said.

"Where's Jon? I want to go home today." He tried to push himself into a sitting position, but fell back with a gasp.

"Son, what's wrong with you? You're too weak to get up yet."

"Yeah," he agreed with a sigh. "But I need to get out of here."

"Why?" Patience said.

"To take care of you and Tommy," he replied frowning at her.

Her heart beat with joy. He wanted to take care of her? What did he mean? She opened her mouth to ask him when he supplied the answer.

"I promised to protect you from the general."

A promise? The general? No, not what she'd hoped for. "You've already done that, Jim, and suffered for it. There's no need to worry about us any longer." She was determined to hide her disappointment. She certainly wasn't going to be pitied.

"What's wrong with you, Patience? It's not over."

"Of course it is. We're back home. He won't bother us again." She nodded at both Megan and Jim. "I'm going back to my room to gather my things. Mother and Tommy and I will be out of your hair in a couple of hours."

"No!" Jim protested.

Megan looked startled.

Patience hid her resentment of his one-word response. "Yes. We need to return to our normal life."

"There's just one problem with that plan, Patience," Jim said.

"What's that?"

"The general isn't dead."

A shudder ran through Patience. She'd avoided thinking about that. "I know," she whispered.

"So you have to stay at the ranch to be safe," Jim added as if that explanation would make everything clear.

"For how long, Jim? Should we move in permanently? I don't think your parents would want that. And neither would I!"

Megan looked from one to the other. "Patience, why don't you stay for a week? Then we can discuss what would be best," she suggested. "We wouldn't want Jim's suffering to be for naught." She smiled at Patience. "Believe me, you and Tommy and your mother won't be a problem. Your mother has already become fast friends with Mildred, Red's wife."

Patience didn't want to accept Megan's gracious invitation. But she owed Jim at least that much. And maybe by the end of a week she could figure out how to protect her son from his father. "I appreciate your invitation, Megan. I guess we could stay a few days."

Both Megan and Jim gave sighs of relief.

"But I have to learn to protect us by myself. Jim isn't responsible for us." She looked directly at him. "I owe you a lot for rescuing us this time."

He shook his head. "I think my owing you for my life is a little more important than my helping you."

Megan turned to stare at Jim. "What do you mean? Did she save your life?"

"Nothing. He's exaggerating."

Jim gave her a hard look. "I don't think so. When the general and his lieutenants attacked us, I told Patience to go on with Tommy. She ignored me. When one of the lieutenants snuck around behind me and had me in his sights, Patience shot him just before he shot, knocking his aim off. Otherwise, he would've hit me in the heart.''

"You don't know that. Maybe he was a poor shot!" Patience insisted.

"I saw him shoot that day I trained the troops. He hit every target dead-on.''

Patience had no response to that. Besides, she didn't have a chance to say anything before Megan threw her arms around her and hugged her tightly. "I can never thank you enough, child.''

"I killed him," Patience muttered. "I need to tell the sheriff.''

"That won't be a problem. You were saving Jim's life.''

"I've never shot anyone or anything before," Patience added. "I feel like I did something wrong.''

Megan hugged her again. "No, you did something very, very right. You may have taken a life, but it was in order to save another. To save yours and Tommy's, as well." She stepped back wiping her eyes. "Thank you.''

Patience was embarrassed. And she still felt as if she'd done something wrong. That moment was going to haunt her for a long time.

"I need to go gather my things." She hurried from the room.

Megan drew a deep breath before she said to Jim, "I think I embarrassed her, but we owe her so much."

"Yeah. I looked down the barrel of that guy's gun and knew I was dead. It took me a minute to realize he'd been shot. Then he fell facedown in the snow." He gave a soft chuckle. "Patience has always been hard to order around. I was really grateful for that trait."

"Yes, definitely."

"Will Dad be in to see me this evening?"

"He'll want to. It depends when they get in. But if he doesn't come tonight, he'll be in first thing in the morning. And he promised Drew he'd tell you that Drew begged to go with him."

"Drew? He's too young to go!"

"That's what I thought about you, too," Megan said with a smile. "I think I'll head home. You don't mind, do you, Jim?"

"Of course not. Thanks for being here and keeping an eye on Patience—and for convincing her to stay awhile."

"We'll do our best, Jim," Megan told him as she kissed his cheek.

She left him with a wave and headed for Patience's room to take her home with her.

WHEN THE RANDALL MEN and the sheriff got far enough down the mountain trail to see the two trucks and trailers waiting for them, they picked up their pace.

Chad muttered, "I never thought I'd be so glad to see a cushioned seat. I must be out of shape."

"You're not out of shape for your age," Jake said. "You're just getting old."

"I'd argue with you if I didn't think I might creak when I get off this horse."

Pete, who was riding right behind Chad, said, "It's not your age as much as it is you were worried. Worrying about our kids makes us old."

"You got that right," Griff joined in.

"Well, I think we can all agree on that," Brett said.

"Makes me glad I never married and had kids," Sheriff Metzger said.

Jake looked down at the two trucks. "I sure hope B.J. drove one of those trucks. I've missed her."

When they got to the bottom of the trail, they

saw that B.J. was indeed one of the drivers. The other was Red.

"Red! What are you doing here?" Brett asked.

Jake, with his arms around B.J., asked, "Couldn't you find someone else to drive the second truck?"

"Too many people," Red assured him. "You've been missed."

Jake smiled, but he turned his attention to the sheriff. "Metzger, you'll come to the house for dinner, won't you? There are things that need to be addressed."

The sheriff nodded. Everyone was thinking about the bodies that needed to be dealt with. "You bet."

"Well, let's get the horses loaded." Jake started the process, opening the door of the four-horse trailer, while the sheriff did the same to the two-horse trailer.

"Griff," B.J. said, "Your wife will be at the house by the time we get there."

"Good. Is she speaking to me? Camille wasn't too happy about my heading off into the mountains."

Jake frowned. "You didn't tell us she was upset."

"She'll get over it. Besides, I needed to be with you all at a time like this."

"Any more word on Jim?" Chad asked.

B.J. nodded. "He's recovering nicely from the surgery. Everything looks real good."

"Is Megan at the house?" Chad asked B.J. as they settled into the truck.

"Yes. She's helping Patience settle in."

"So she agreed to stay at the house?"

"Yes. Since Jim is afraid that Kane fellow may still be coming for Patience and Tommy, he wanted them protected. Until he's out of the hospital, she's promised to stay with us."

Chad nodded. Then B.J. added, "She saved his life."

"What? How?"

B.J. told him the story as Megan had told it to her.

When she finished, Chad could only say, "We certainly owe her a lot."

THE TABLE IN the Randall kitchen could seat as many as twenty people. When Patience came down to dinner, she stood to one side, out of the flow of people, wondering what she should do.

"There you are, Patience," her mother said, as if their being in the Randall kitchen was normal. "I told Mildred you'd mix up your special dressing for the salad."

"You don't mind, do you, Patience? I tasted it at one of the potluck dinners and I've been meaning to ask you for the recipe," Mildred, Red's wife and B.J.'s aunt, said.

Patience agreed at once. Anything was better than everyone praising her as a hero. Megan had told them that Patience had saved Jim's life. Patience tried to explain that she owed Jim for his help, not the other way around.

She moved over to the cabinet and told Mildred what ingredients she needed. Mildred was a kind soul and soon put her at ease.

"Now, we're going to call the younger ones to dinner, so the men can have room to eat when they get back," Mildred explained.

Patience dreaded facing the men who had ridden into the mountains after them. Especially the sheriff. She would have to find a time to talk privately with him.

She'd thought if she got Tommy back, everything would be right with her world. How wrong she'd been. Not only did she still need to worry about Kane trying to get Tommy, but she also had to deal with her feelings for Jim.

She missed his strength, his calm appraisal of

situations. She missed his warmth, a feeling that surrounded her when she was with him. He made her a stronger, happier person. Most of all, she loved his sense of humor.

She blinked rapidly to dispel the tears that filled her eyes.

Megan moved to her side. "Everything's okay, Patience, I promise."

Patience gave her a smile and nodded. She knew differently, but she wasn't going to tell Megan that.

When the first round of dinner was announced, Tommy came running to the table. His grandmother demanded a kiss, and Tommy willingly gave her one.

"You want one, too, Mommy?" Tommy asked.

"That would be nice." Patience smiled at her little boy.

Tommy threw himself into her arms and kissed her cheek as she bent down. "I'm having so much fun! Davy has some video games. He's teaching me how to play."

"I'm glad, sweetie. Don't forget your manners during dinner, okay?"

He grinned. "Okay."

She watched him follow Davy to the table.

Her heart swelled with pride when he did as Elizabeth told him. He was a good little boy. And Kane was a bastard.

Thanks to Jim, she had her little boy back.

She helped with the serving, making herself useful where she could. It took her mind off her problems. The meal was almost over when the back door opened and the four Randall fathers, plus the sheriff and Griffin Randall, entered. Immediately the wives went to greet their husbands.

Even Camille, who had protested Griff's decision to accompany his cousins, threw herself into Griff's embrace. Patience couldn't hold back a smile. It was good to see the love that existed between these couples.

After the greetings, the women quickly cleared the table and placed clean dishes on it. All except Megan. She remained in a corner, talking with her husband.

When they finished talking, Chad stepped to Red's side and conferred with him. Then, to Patience's surprise, Jim's father turned to her.

"Patience, Megan's told me about you saving Jim's life. We can never thank you enough for that."

"Mr. Randall, I owe Jim for saving me and

Tommy from Kane. You don't owe me any-thing.''

"You're a gracious woman, Patience. But we still owe you. Megan and I are going in to see Jim now. Do you want to come with us?"

Patience blushed. "Oh, no, I talked to him today. I'll let you have some time alone with him. I think he's doing very well."

"We Randalls are fast healers," Chad assured her with a smile.

"I'm glad."

"Yeah. Any messages for Jim?"

"You can tell him again how grateful I am."

Chad smiled and left.

Half an hour later Patience asked the sheriff, who'd just finished his meal, if she could talk to him.

He agreed and suggested they use Jake's of-fice.

She followed him, her knees shaking.

Chapter Nine

Once Patience was seated in one of the big leather chairs in front of Jake's desk, she clasped her hands tightly together. Her voice strained, she said, "Sheriff, I killed a man."

Sheriff Metzger had been a law officer for a long time and had seen his share of crime. Calmly he asked, "Did you?"

"Yes. We were trying to get away from Kane and his men. We were almost home when they found us and started shooting at us. This man had snuck up on Jim and was going to kill him. I couldn't let him do that. I shot him." She let out a sigh. "Are you going to file charges against me?"

"Well, seeing as how you didn't seek these men out with the intent to kill and that you had been fired on first, no. All you did was try to protect Jim and Tommy and yourself. I'll interview Jim and if his story matches yours there will be no charges.''

"Are you sure? I feel so bad about it."

"Patience, life is harsh. No decent person seeks to end someone else's life. But there are times when you have no choice. This was one of those times. And if, as we think, Kane is still alive, it's possible you'll face him again. I hope you'll seek legal recourse at once so that he can't get hold of Tommy again.''

"Do you think I have a chance to get custody of Tommy?"

"Yes, I do. His father is obviously not a stable man. Go to Nick Randall and ask for his help.''

"He would be very expensive, but..." She began considering her options, hoping she could do as the sheriff suggested.

"Just talk to him. I'm sure he'll offer you some good advice.''

"Thank you, Sheriff Metzger, for talking to me. I feel better now.''

"I'm glad you're staying with the Randalls for a while, where you'll be safe. I'll let you know right away if I get any hint that Joseph Kane is back in town.''

"Thank you." She'd have to let the sheriff know when she moved back home, as she fully intended to do in a few days…

JIM WAS USING his left hand to feed himself. He was managing okay, except for the peas. Balancing the small peas on his fork took more talent than he had, so he abandoned that part of his meal.

When he heard the door open, he looked up and was pleased to see his parents. "Dad! I'm glad you're back."

Chad didn't hesitate to hug his son. But he was careful of his injured shoulder. "Did Jon check you today?"

"Yeah. He said I might go home tomorrow."

"That's wonderful, dear." Megan went to him and gave him a hug, as well.

"Is Patience at the ranch?" Jim asked.

"Yeah," Chad answered. "I thanked her for saving your life. Your mother told me."

"Yeah."

"We found two dead bodies." Chad looked at his son, waiting for his response.

"Those were two of the general's lieutenants. They caught us the last day. I shot one and Patience shot the other."

"Did you see the general escape?"

"Yeah. He was with the one I shot, and I think he saw the other one fall. That's when he rode off in the other direction."

"Toward the cabin?"

Jim frowned. "Yeah. Why? Did he use the cabin?"

"I think he burned the cabin. We saw the smoke the afternoon before, which would've been while you were coming down."

"Damn him! I'm sorry, Dad. Patience, Tommy and I spent that last night in the cabin so we could have a hot meal and get a little rest. Patience had been up all night the day before."

"It was a good plan, son, and it worked. You got down safely."

"Thanks to Patience. The kids will really miss going to the cabin this summer, though."

"Maybe we'll rebuild and you can do some hammering."

"That's a deal, Dad," Jim said.

THE NEXT MORNING, after she'd made sure Tommy had eaten breakfast and was happily playing with Davy, Patience came downstairs. "Is anyone going to town today?" she asked.

Megan immediately told her she was going in

to pick up Jim. "Did you want to come with me?"

"Well, I need to pick up my car and I have some errands to run."

"Then of course I'll be glad to give you a ride. Or I could drive you around if you need to shop or something."

Patience knew Megan was curious about her errands, but she didn't want to tell the Randalls that she was going to go see their cousin, Nick Randall.

After an awkward pause Megan said, "I'll be ready to leave in about fifteen minutes, if that's all right."

"Yes, I'll be ready."

On the ride into town, Megan didn't ask any more questions. Patience was grateful. Nick Randall was the best lawyer around. Patience wasn't sure she could afford him, but she had to start there. She needed to make sure that Tommy was legally hers. She should've done it long before now.

Once Megan had dropped her off at her house, Patience drove her own car to the main street of Rawhide and parked. Then she entered Nick's law office, which was across the street from the general store.

"May I help you?" the receptionist asked.

"I'd like to see Nick Randall."

"Do you have an appointment?"

Patience stared at her. "An appointment? Uh, no."

"He's not in the office this morning. Could you come back this afternoon?"

Like she had a choice. Patience nodded. "What time this afternoon?"

"Just a minute. I'll check with him." The receptionist picked up the phone and dialed a number. "Mr. Randall? What time could you take an appointment this afternoon?"

Patience stood there, feeling like an idiot for thinking she could just walk in and see the lawyer.

"Ma'am, what's your name?"

Hurriedly she replied, "Patience Anderson."

The woman repeated her name into the phone. "Oh. Yes, sir, of course." She hung up the phone and said, "Mr. Randall is available now. He'll be right down."

Now Patience was thoroughly embarrassed. She knew Nick lived on the floor above his office, but she hadn't meant to intrude on his personal life. "I don't want to disturb him. I can come back later." Before she finished, a door behind the receptionist opened.

"Now, why would you want to do that, Patience, when I have time on my hands this morning?" Nick Randall asked with a grin.

"But you must've had plans," Patience protested. "I didn't mean to—"

"Don't be silly. Come on in." He escorted her into his private office. "My wife wanted me to baby-sit our little boy this morning, but he's taking a nap." He put a baby monitor receiver on his desk. "We'll use the monitor. If he wakes up, I'll have to go upstairs for a minute."

"Okay," she agreed.

"By the way, I'm glad to hear you got your little boy back. Is he all right?"

"He's great. Jim was wounded, though. He's going home from the hospital today, so he's recovering quickly."

"I heard that. My brother called last night. I was going to go see Jim today."

Patience smiled politely.

"Now, what do you need to talk to me about?"

"I don't know how much you charge, Nick, but I'm in need of a good lawyer."

"Tell me the problem. We'll worry about payment later."

"Well," she began, "Tommy is my sister's child, and Joseph Kane is his father. Kane left town as soon as Faith died. We neither saw nor heard from him until he came back last week and abducted Tommy. I've raised Tommy since he was born. But because I hadn't legally adopted him, the sheriff said he couldn't do anything about Tommy's abduction."

"I'm not sure I agree with him, but obviously you want to remedy that situation. Do you want complete guardianship of Tommy?"

"Yes," Patience said with relief. "Can that be done?"

"Tell me what Mr. Kane was doing with Tommy when you found them. I heard you went after him by yourself."

She nodded. "Yes. Kane was making Tommy stand at attention in the snow. Every time the boy moved, Joe would slap him quite hard. He'd just knocked him down for the third time when I entered the camp."

"Physical abuse," Nick said, and made a note.

"Yes. If Jim hadn't come—" She broke off and covered her face with her hands.

"What do you believe would have happened?"

"Kane decided he wanted to marry me and have more sons so he'd have a bigger army to command."

"He told you this?"

"I believe he would have forced himself on me. Thankfully, Jim had come and he got Tommy and me out of there."

"Well, thank goodness Jim showed up."

"But then he was shot. I—"

"Hello, Nick." Jim's voice startled them both as he entered the room.

"Jim, I just heard you were getting out this morning. How are you?" Nick asked, obviously not as startled by Jim's presence as Patience was.

"I'm doing well, Nick. I know I shouldn't have interrupted, but I needed to know what Patience was up to."

Patience stiffened. "You could've asked me."

"Mom said she did, and you didn't tell her anything." Jim sat down in the chair next to her. "Sorry, I can't stand for too long."

"Of course, Jim," Nick said. "But Patience is entitled to have this discussion in private if she wants. Patience?"

"I don't mind Jim knowing what I'm doing, but I can't see any real need for his presence."

"I want to make sure Nick understands that I'll pay the bill for his work. He's the best," Jim told her.

Patience tried to maintain her dignity, but she was growing angry. "I'm going to arrange a payment plan with Nick. I don't need your money."

"I owe you my life, Patience. How much do you think that's worth?"

Nick's eyebrows soared and his gaze traveled back and forth between the two combatants before he broke in. "I've assured Patience I'm willing to help her. It's an interesting case. So, Jim, you don't have to worry about it."

"But I think she should've talked to me first," Jim argued, which caused Nick's brows to soar again.

"Tommy is my child," Patience said. "I appreciate your help, but that does not put you in charge, Jim. And I promise I won't call on you again."

"Do you think you're going to prevent that madman from trying to get his son again?" Jim asked.

"No. But I'm going to have the law on my side the next time."

"The law moves slowly. Kane could kidnap Tommy and carry him out of state before you could get Sheriff Metzger to act. But I don't have to wait. And I love Tommy, too. I'll be there for you."

Patience closed her eyes and gritted her teeth. Once she had herself under control, she said to Nick, "What do I have to do?"

"I'll need to take your statement about Mr. Kane—what he's done for his son, or to his son. I'll need the specifics of how you can afford to care for him. Some character references for you. When do you want to do that?"

"I'm prepared to do any of that at your convenience, Nick. I want to have this issue settled as quickly as possible."

"Well, we can—"

"Anyone in my family will provide character references for Patience," Jim said insistently. "Mom's waiting in your outer office. She can—"

"Your mother scarcely knows me!" Patience protested.

"Why won't you let us help you?"

"Because I can manage on my own!" she returned.

Nick stood and moved to Jim's side. "Let me help you to the outer office. I want to get started on Patience's case at once. I'll let you know what you can do to help us."

Jim wasn't strong enough to fight Nick. Not today. But he wasn't happy being escorted out. When Nick had him outside his office, he said, "She's being hardheaded, Nick. She needs help."

"Probably. But we have to give her a little room. You can't take away her freedom of choice."

"What's wrong?" Megan asked. She'd gotten to her feet when the two men appeared.

Nick grinned. "Patience and Jim seem to have a lot of friction between them." He winked at Megan.

Jim saw the wink and didn't understand its significance. "She's just being difficult. She thinks she can handle everything by herself."

"Is Patience upset?" Megan asked.

"A little," Nick said.

"Let me go talk to her so she'll come back to the house tonight. That's important." She walked into Nick's office even as her son protested.

Jim finally apologized to Nick for interrupting his meeting with Patience, but he believed Patience would let her pride get in the way. "She doesn't have much patience, in spite of her name."

"I see," Nick said, a grin on his face.

"Why is that funny?" Jim demanded.

"It reminds me of when I was courting my wife."

"No! No, I'm not…well, maybe eventually, but she needs time to settle her business."

"And that's what I'm going to help her do," Nick promised. "We may be able to get legal custody pretty quickly if the docket isn't full. I'm going to try for the first of next week."

"That'd be great," Jim said.

Megan came out of Nick's office. "We can go now, Jim. Patience needs to talk some more with Nick. She'll be home for dinner, though. She promised."

Jim gave his mother a dark look and muttered a goodbye to Nick.

When they were in the truck, Megan said, "Jim, you've got to remember that Patience is not a member of our family. She gets to make her own decisions."

"I was trying to help her, Mom."

"You were trying to make decisions for her," his mother said. "Your father tried that a few times with me, too. But Patience has provided for her mother and her nephew for three years now, making her own decisions. You can't take over her life."

"I'm not trying to," Jim protested. "I'm just trying to help her."

"Well, until you marry her, find another way to help her."

"What? Mom, I'm not going to… I mean, we haven't talked about… How did you know?" he finally asked.

"Your father and I did quite a bit of arguing when we first met. It just reminded me of that."

Jim sighed. "I haven't said anything to her yet. She may still be mad about what happened at college."

"I don't understand what made you two break up. You've never told me."

Jim gave her a wry look. "And I'm not going to now, either. But I'll try to work things out as soon as I can."

Chapter Ten

Patience turned up at the Randall house for dinner as she'd promised. Immediately she started helping put dinner on the table for the children.

When Tommy came downstairs, he ran into her arms. "Where you been, Mommy? I missed you. Grandma said you went to town. Did you bring me something?"

"Sure. I brought you a kiss. I missed you, too." She picked him up and kissed his soft cheek. "Did you play with Davy all day?"

"Yes, and I played with Jim, too. He's hurted and he has to stay in bed. His mommy said so."

"I know, sweetie, but he's going to get better." She only hoped she was right. Today he'd seemed as impatient as he always told her she was.

After the children had eaten, she helped clean the table.

"You're a hard worker, young lady," Mildred said.

"I'm glad to help. The last thing you needed was three more mouths to feed."

"We're glad to have you. That Tommy is cute as can be, and he keeps Davy occupied," Mildred said. "And your mom and I have become good friends. She's showing me how to make lace."

"Yes, she's very good at that."

The door to the kitchen opened and Patience looked up. Jim came in, flanked by his parents and his brother. She immediately turned her back and began stirring a pot of beans on the stove.

She was able to stay busy helping serve the meal. Then there was nothing left to do but take a seat at the table. That was when she realized she'd made a critical mistake.

Everyone was seated except for Red, Mildred and her. They always sat in the same seats. Which left her a vacant seat right next to Jim. She desperately looked around for another option, but there was none.

Jim smiled at her. "Come on, Patience. You're holding up dinner."

She blushed. The last thing she wanted to do

was create problems for the Randalls. She took her place and the blessing was asked. Then they all began talking and passing platters of food.

Jim leaned toward her. "I owe you an apology."

She shook her head but said nothing. He didn't pursue the conversation, but he asked her to cut his steak for him. "My right arm is still sore," he explained.

She hurriedly began cutting his steak. After all, it was her fault he'd been injured. When she finished, she withdrew again. She concentrated on her own meal, hoping to finish as soon as possible.

"What's your hurry? Are you going somewhere tonight?" Jim asked, frowning.

"No! I want to help with the dishes."

"Not tonight. We need to talk."

She stiffened. "You are not my boss, Jim. You need to go back to bed, anyway, so you'll get better."

"Not until we've had a talk. It's dangerous for you to run around town by yourself. You shouldn't have gotten your car. I'm sure Kane knows your car, since you've had it since you went off to college."

"I keep my doors locked."

"Yeah, and then you get out of the car. So how safe are you then?"

"Jim, I can't hide forever. Besides, he probably won't come here again."

"I'm just saying you shouldn't run around by yourself. I can't get back in the saddle for a while, so I can go with you as protection."

"No!" she protested sharply, causing conversation to die around the table. With everyone staring at her, she stammered, "I'm t-trying to convince Jim that I don't need protection now."

After an awkward pause, Chad said, "Why not? Do you think Kane has given up?"

"No, but you said you had found his camp deserted. Plus, two of his lieutenants are dead, the third injured. I assume he doesn't have any followers anymore."

"And that means he won't be interested in his son?" Jake asked.

"I don't think he really wants Tommy with him. He wanted more soldiers. And he lost all the soldiers he had because of me and Tommy."

"She's got a point," Brett agreed. Both Jim and his father glared at Brett and he ducked his head.

"I think he'll be mad and want revenge," Jim

said. "You got the best of him the first time. He'll be determined to pay you back."

"Oh!" Megan exclaimed, drawing everyone's attention. "Did you ever find out what those strange coins were? The tin ones with the 30p stamped on them?"

"Yeah," Jim said. "Kane had them made. He believes God betrayed him when Faith, his wife, died. The 30p stands for the thirty pieces of silver Judas was paid for betraying Jesus. Kane thinks he shouldn't have to pay for anything he wants, because God owes him."

"His logic is a little warped, since he's the reason Faith died," Anna said quietly, anger in her voice.

"It's a wonder he doesn't blame Tommy," B.J. said.

As if a light clicked on in Patience's head, she said, "Maybe he does, subconsciously. His behavior toward Tommy was fairly brutal."

"Then we'd best make sure he doesn't get his hands on him again," Chad said with a firm nod.

There was agreement all around the table. "I won't let him," Patience assured them, trying to let them know that she didn't expect any more sacrifices from the Randalls.

Marilyn Anderson said, "Well, of course he won't get Tommy as long as we're here."

Patience pressed her lips together to hold back a groan. Her mother was one of those women who expects to be protected. Now that her husband and oldest child were gone, she expected Patience to take care of her. "Mom, we're only staying a few days. Then we're going home."

Everyone looked at Jim, as if they expected him to do something. "We'll talk about it," he said, not looking at Patience.

She wanted to tell him he was wrong. It was her decision and she'd already made it. But not in front of the senior Randalls. They'd all been very kind and she didn't want to offend them.

With a shrug she picked up her fork and continued eating. In spite of what Jim thought, she could be patient sometimes.

As soon as the meal was over, Patience leaped to her feet, planning on busying herself with cleaning up while Jim left the kitchen.

But Jim was prepared. He grabbed her hand and wouldn't let go when she tugged. "I want to show you something at the barn."

She stared at him as if he was crazy. "It's cold out."

"So wear a coat. It won't be too cold in the barn."

"I need to help with the dishes, Jim." She tugged again.

"You can help with them when we get back," he said. "You don't mind, do you, Mildred?"

"Of course not, Jim. We'll manage. You go ahead, young lady. You've worked harder than anyone else since you came here."

Feeling trapped, Patience finally nodded, adding, "I won't be but a minute." She hoped Jim got the message.

Jim nodded, as if agreeing with her, which was a surprise. Maybe he'd been serious when he said he just wanted to show her something. She relaxed a little, glad she didn't have to fight another battle.

Drew, at the other end of the table, leaned forward and said, "What do you want to show her, Jim? I can walk her down there while you go rest. It won't be a problem."

"No!" Jim glared at his brother.

Chad halted anything else Jim might've said. "That's good of you, Drew, but I need to talk to you about tomorrow's work. Let's go to Jake's office."

Drew looked surprised but nodded.

Jim looked relieved, which made Patience suspicious again.

Before she could ask any more questions, Jim stood. He wavered momentarily. Patience sprang up to support him before he fell.

"I'm okay," he said. "I need to remember to take things slowly." He nodded to his mother. Then, still holding Patience's hand, he turned toward the back door.

"My jacket is hanging in the mudroom. Where's yours?" Patience asked. She wasn't going to be blamed for him catching a cold.

"It's out there, too." Jim released her hand when they reached the mudroom and let her help him into his coat. She was surprised by his docility. It made her look at him sharply. Was he exhausted?

"Jim, surely this can wait until you're feeling stronger. I'm going to be here a couple more days."

"Don't fuss over me. I'm fine."

Her concern hadn't made him happy. Well, too bad.

He led the way to the back door. The minute he opened it, they both felt a cold gust of wind. "Feels like another norther is blowing through," he said with a frown. "I'm glad we're not still up there."

"Yeah, me, too. Though the cabin was a good shelter," she said, remembering the night they'd spent there.

"Oh. I guess no one's told you. Someone burned the cabin down."

She came to a halt before they were even off the porch. "Someone? You mean Kane? He was the only one in the area, wasn't he? How terrible! I'm so sorry, Jim. I know how much your family enjoyed going there in the summer."

"Dad says we're going to rebuild it this summer."

"I'll help."

Jim sighed. Then he leaned over and kissed her.

She froze. His touch was so warm, so exciting. It brought back memories she needed to forget. "Don't do that!"

He ignored her order. "Let's get to the barn so we can shut out the wind." Grabbing her hand again, he stepped down off the porch.

He'd chosen the mother barn, so called because any animal, horse or cow that was experiencing difficulties in giving birth was brought to this barn. And he happened to know, since he'd quizzed his dad earlier in the day, that it was empty right now.

They rushed in, pushing the door closed behind them, and Jim clicked on the overhead light.

"Are there any animals in here?" Patience asked.

"Not right now."

"So what did you want to show me?"

Jim sat down on a bale of hay. "Sorry, I need to sit down."

When he didn't respond to her question, she prodded him. "Jim? You haven't answered me."

"I said I wanted to show you something so we could have some privacy. I don't like to grovel in front of my family."

Rather than joining him on the bale of hay, as he was indicating by patting a place beside him, she took a step back.

"What are you talking about?"

"I owe you an apology. I shouldn't have burst in on you today at Nick's office. That was your business and I tried to make it mine."

"Thank you," she said, pleased by his apology.

"But you're going to have to change your ways, Patience."

That remark wasn't to her liking, and it didn't sound like an apology. "I beg your pardon?"

"Honey, I'm not trying to be difficult, but you can't run around by yourself, even here in Rawhide. That man presents a real danger, and you know it."

"He's not in Rawhide. I suspect he's long gone, trying to find more young gullible men he can enlist in a new army. He won't have time for me and Tommy." She prayed she was right.

"And you're willing to risk Tommy's safety?"

"I'm going to protect Tommy!"

"How are you going to do that? If Kane finds you out on your own, he'll subdue you, force you to lead him to Tommy."

"Well?" Jim prodded when she said nothing.

"I'm buying a gun."

Jim sighed. "Look, Patience, I'd be the last one to think a gun is a bad idea. Without you having a gun, I'd be dead. But are you sure you can kill Kane? And what if it's in front of Tommy?"

"Stop! I don't have a choice. I have to protect my son."

"You do have a choice. You can let us help you." He grabbed her hands when he reached her. "Come on, Patience. We'll help you."

"No. I have to stand on my own two feet. I'm not part of your family."

"Dammit! Patience, anyone in Rawhide would protect you. You know that."

"Everyone in Rawhide is kin to *you!*"

"You're exaggerating, Patience. We're a big family, but everyone isn't kin to us." He gave her a smile.

She didn't return his lighthearted response. "I have to do this on my own." She turned to go.

Again he grabbed her hand. "Come on, Patience. I care about you and Tommy. You know that." He pulled her and she fell against him.

He wrapped his arms tightly around her, even though he grimaced at the pain. His lips covered hers and swept her back to three years ago, when Jim was her world. She'd wanted him, wanted to make love with him, but there had been too much going on in her life.

Now, she couldn't. Or maybe she could. He'd helped her. She could give him what he wanted, couldn't she? "Jim, I...I owe you. If you want me, I—"

Jim stepped away from her as if she were on

fire. He stared at her. "I can't believe you said that, Patience Anderson! What's happened to you?"

"What's happened to me? I'm trying to survive, protect my family." She fought back tears.

"And you have no respect for me? You think I helped you, or tried to help you, because I just wanted to sleep with you?" He was livid, his face red.

Patience swallowed. Hard. "I thought—"

"I don't want to hear it!" Jim roared. "I don't trade help for sex!"

Patience turned and ran out of the barn. When she reached the porch of the house, she wiped her tears away with her palms before she went inside and hurried to her room.

CHAD STRODE INTO the barn, looking for his son. He found Jim sitting on a bale of hay, running his hands through his hair.

"Jim?" he asked. "What happened? Patience came running into the house and went straight to her room."

"I made a mistake," Jim muttered, not looking up.

"What do you mean? What mistake?"

"I kissed her."

Chad released the breath he'd been holding. "That's all that happened? You kissed her? Why did she act so...so upset?"

Jim began pacing the barn floor, his right hand in his jeans pocket for support. "I kissed her and she offered to sleep with me as payment for my helping her!"

"Why would she do that?" Chad asked.

"We were in love during college. But Patience told me she wouldn't sleep with me unless we were engaged."

"And that was so horrible?"

"No! But I didn't like being pushed into it. So I got stubborn. Told her I was too young to be tied down. I held out as long as I could. Two weeks later I called her. Her roommate said she'd gone home and she wasn't coming back. I called her, but she didn't want to talk to me. She just said she never wanted to see me again."

"Was that when her sister died?"

"Yes, but I didn't find out about all that until later. I made up my mind to put her out of my life. I purposely didn't ask about her."

"Son, sounds like you and Patience have a lot to work out. It might be best to do some talking before you try anything else."

"Yeah, but even if we haven't worked out the

past, I never suggested she should pay me back with sex.''

''I believe you, son. I know you wouldn't do that to Patience. But if she refuses to let you stay close to her, we'll have a hard time helping her if she has trouble.''

''I know.''

''Has she figured out how she'll protect Tommy and herself?''

''Yeah. She says she's going to buy a gun. But that's not the answer. Hell, it shouldn't have come to a shooting match between her and Kane.'' His jaw hardened. ''I'm planning to stick to her like glue, no matter what she says.''

''Do you think you'll get her to agree?''

''Dad, I won't take no for an answer.''

Chapter Eleven

When she got up, Patience took one look at herself in the mirror the next morning and wanted to go back to bed and hide under the covers. She'd shed a lot of tears last night after she'd gone to bed. She'd cried for her past, her present and her future. And they all included Jim.

She'd shoved him out of her life three years ago. After realizing what a mistake her sister had made, she'd been determined to control her own life. What a joke! No one can control what happens in life.

Last night her offer to have sex with him as payment for his help had really been an attempt to justify her own desires. But she'd only offended Jim, and again she was left alone.

And the future? She had no future with Jim. She'd already blown her chances.

She was late getting downstairs. She found Tommy playing with Davy's video games in the living room. It took several minutes to get Tommy to put down his controller and give her a morning kiss, but she persisted.

"I know you love playing, Tommy, but you can give me a minute or two. I have to go back into town today. I want you to mind Grandma and go to her if you need anything, okay?"

"Okay." His gaze had returned to the television. She gave him another kiss and let him go back to the game. He probably wouldn't like it when they moved back home. No games and no Davy.

Breakfast was already over in the Randall kitchen. But as soon as she came through the door, Mildred and Red both jumped to their feet.

"We saved you some breakfast," Mildred said with a smile. In no time, a plate of eggs and bacon and hot biscuits were in front of her.

"Thank you so much. I had a rough night last night, which made me oversleep."

"Don't worry, child," Red said, patting her shoulder. "It happens to all of us."

As soon as she finished eating, she excused herself, explaining that she had an appointment with Nick. She wanted to ask about Jim, how he was this morning, but she didn't think she had the right to ask.

Pulling on her coat, she went outside and headed for her car. As she approached she realized someone was in the front passenger seat. Her first thought was that Kane had found her already. Then she recognized Jim.

She opened her car door. "You idiot! What are you doing?" She slid behind the wheel. "You scared me to death."

Jim, slumped in the seat, didn't move. "I'm waiting for you."

"That much is obvious. But why?"

"I told you it's not safe for you to run around alone. With my injury I can't work on the ranch for a while. So I'm providing you with an armed guard."

Patience's eyes widened. "Armed? What do you mean?"

He straightened and shoved back his coat. There was a leather holster strapped on his body.

"You really don't think anything is necessary, do you?"

"Why were you scared?"

Okay, he'd made his point. "But it's unfair of me to expect you to follow me around all day. I'll be at Nick's office the entire morning."

"I know. I brought a blanket so I can keep warm in the car if you're inside a long time. What do you have planned for this afternoon?"

"I thought I'd go home and clean up, do some grocery shopping for when we move back in."

"That's the first place Kane will look for you," Jim said, his voice hard.

"We won't go back until I have a gun. But we can't live with your family forever."

"Until you get that gun, I'm going to be your shadow, so get used to it."

She couldn't force him out of her car. And she'd admit that his presence gave her more confidence. She didn't deserve his concern, but she sure wasn't going to fight it.

They drove in silence to Nick's office.

When she parked the car and started to get out, he didn't move. "Why don't you come in and wait in the outer office?"

"I don't want to embarrass you."

"Jim, stop being a martyr. You know you're not an embarrassment. Come in and stay warm." She got out, refusing to wait to see if he took her up on the offer. If he wanted to sit outside in the cold, that was his choice.

She heard his door open, but she didn't turn around.

Inside, the same young woman was behind the reception desk. The immediate thought that she'd keep Jim entertained brought a surge of jealousy that took Patience by surprise. Shame on her. She'd lost Jim twice already. And she thought she should have a third opportunity?

"Third time's the charm," she muttered.

"Ma'am? I'm sorry, I didn't hear you."

Patience managed a smile. "I was talking to myself. I'm here to see Nick. Patience Anderson."

"Yes, I remember. He's waiting for you."

Patience nodded and entered Nick's office.

Nick had good news. "I got your hearing on the docket for Monday. We should have an answer, a favorable one, I hope, by Wednesday."

"That's wonderful, Nick! Thank you so much."

"I'm glad you're happy. But I'm worried about you being out on your own. You will be careful, won't you?"

"I'm not on my own. I have an armed guard in the outer office."

Nick appeared startled. Then his features relaxed into a smile. "Jim?"

"Yes, he insists."

"Good for him. Well, let's get started. Maybe you'll be free by lunch."

JIM PASSED the next few hours reading the magazines Nick had in his reception area. The magazines for men covered ranching business and sports. When he finished all those, he picked up a women's magazine. Anything to keep him occupied so the woman behind the desk didn't try to flirt with him.

She wasn't ugly. In fact, she was quite beautiful, but his total lack of interest in her pointed out to him that he was in love with Patience and no one else. He smiled as he remembered his dad talking about the first time he'd met his mom.

His uncle Jake had invited three female interior designers to the ranch to update the house. In reality, he was looking for wives for his brothers. He had every intention of marrying off Pete first. But Pete was already in love with Janie, though they'd broken up.

Thank goodness, because when Chad saw Megan, he was taken at once. Used to being chased, her aloofness intrigued him. And before long, he knew he was hooked. But he vowed to forget her if she wanted Pete, which had been Jake's plan.

Jim smiled at his father's willingness to sacrifice. Controlling life was impossible. As he'd learned when he tried to control Patience. But he'd learned that lesson too late.

Was he really being given another chance? He was having trouble reading her. Her offer of sex in gratitude had thrown him. But he was beginning to wish he'd taken her up on the offer.

The door opened and Patience emerged, with Nick right behind her.

Jim stood and extended his hand to his cousin. "All done?"

"Until Monday. I got us on the docket for Monday afternoon," Nick explained.

"Terrific. I'll tell the sheriff when we drop by to see him."

"Why are we going to do that?" Patience demanded.

"Because we need to stay in close contact with him until we know for sure you're safe. He also has some questions about the shootings." His steady gaze dared her to argue with him. He released his breath when she glanced away.

"Okay."

"Are you going to have lunch at the café first?" Nick asked.

Jim didn't try to make this decision for Patience. He looked at her and waited.

"Yes, I think so." Patience smiled at Nick.

"Mind if I join you? Sarah and her sister Jennifer have gone to Casper to do some shopping. I think they've started Christmas shopping already."

"But it's still October," Jim said.

"Ask Patience. Women plan their shopping the way men plan mergers. But I sure like the results." Nick grinned. He'd been born a Randall but had been adopted and raised as an only son by socialites in Denver. He'd only discovered his birth family a few years ago and found he loved the vigor and affection of his large family.

Jim chuckled. "Yeah, a Randall Christmas is pretty special."

Patience said nothing.

Jim glanced at her and decided to change the subject. He'd started dating her in the early spring and they'd broken up the following fall. She'd never personally experienced a Randall celebration at Christmas except as a resident of Rawhide.

"You hungry?" Jim asked Patience.

"Yes, surprisingly, I am."

"Why surprisingly?" Nick asked.

Jim laughed again. "Red and Mildred were waiting for her this morning. She overslept and they fixed her a special breakfast."

"Ah." Nick nodded in understanding as he moved them toward the door. "Go ahead and close up, Nancy," he told the woman behind the desk.

When they stepped out into the cold air, Nick asked, "Have you ever had Red's chocolate cake? That's something you won't forget too soon. My wife, Sarah, had vowed to stop eating his cake because she said it was too rich—until she found out she was pregnant." He was beaming.

"Nick, that's great!" Jim said. "Congratulations."

"Thanks, Jim. We're excited. Our Bryan is almost two. Sarah's hoping for a little girl. But I told her it's not likely. We Randall's tend to have boys."

Jim nodded in agreement, but Patience laughed. "You two are so macho. I think little girls are wonderful. Steffie is such a sweet little girl," she said, referring to Toby's daughter.

They'd reached the café. It was crowded, as it usually was on a Saturday, but they managed to find a booth in the back.

"Nick, mind if we sit facing the door?" Jim asked as he guided Patience into the booth first. "I don't want any surprises."

"No, of course not. I don't have any rabid enemies right now."

Jim nodded. "Rabid is right. Kane isn't sane."

"That's what I've heard. How did your sister meet him, Patience?"

Patience drew a deep breath. "He came to Rawhide four years ago, doing odd jobs. He even came to church. That's where Faith met him. We didn't know much about him. He swept Faith off her feet. He didn't mention that they'd be leaving as soon as she married him. The letters she sent told us she was very lonely and homesick."

"Yeah," Jim agreed. "I can imagine."

"When she finally came home, she was pregnant and run-down. Faith was older than me, but she was always so gentle. I felt it was my job to protect her." Patience glanced away, unable to face the sympathetic looks of the two men.

"I wanted Jon to check her out at once, but

her husband—he'd come with Faith—forbade her to go to a doctor. I planned to beg Jon to come to our house the moment Joseph left for any period of time, but he didn't. Then, when she started labor, I knew something was wrong. I called Anna. As soon as she got there, she called Jon and did what she could for her.''

"It's not your fault," Jim whispered, hearing the agony in her voice.

"When Jon got there, he managed to deliver the baby with Anna's help. I think we all knew Faith was dying, she'd lost so much blood. They kept working on her, trying. Joseph walked out and we never heard from him again until he abducted Tommy.''

"We're going to remove him from Tommy's life. And yours, too," Nick assured her. "Legally at least.''

"That will help." Patience mustered a slight smile for Nick.

They ordered their meals and kept their conversation on lighter topics. Nick left first, after paying for everyone, insisting on doing so because Patience was his client.

Jim turned to Patience. "What do you want to do after we see the sheriff?''

"I want to check on our house. Get the mail.''

"You know you can't move back yet," Jim said as he stood.

With a sigh, she followed him. "Not yet," she agreed.

He let her precede him out the door, stopping to shake hands with one of his dad's friends. Then he followed Patience until she abruptly stopped. He grabbed her shoulders to avoid running in to her.

"Hey, Patience, give me some warning when you're going to put on the brakes," he said with a laugh.

She didn't respond.

He suddenly noticed how rigid she'd gone. He quickly scanned the area. "What is it? Did you see him?"

"Yes, but...now he's disappeared. He was there and now he isn't. Jim, h-he's back." Her voice trembled.

He wrapped his arms around her, giving her his warmth and strength. "Hang on, honey. Let's get to the sheriff's office."

Patience's paralysis scared her almost as much as thinking she saw Kane. She couldn't allow her body to betray her that way. She had to be ready to fight.

"What if the sheriff doesn't believe me?" Patience asked, panic in her voice.

"He'll believe you, sweetheart."

"But, Jim, maybe I think I saw him because I'm worried." Her hands were trembling and her voice shook.

"Patience, my dad told me there's nothing wrong with being afraid. It's how you handle that fear that counts. And you're going to do just fine." He leaned over and kissed her lips. Then he opened the door to the sheriff's office.

When Sheriff Metzger saw them enter, he stood. "Good to see you both. How are you, Patience?"

"She's a little shaken up. She thinks she saw Joseph Kane on the street across from the café," Jim said.

The sheriff looked at Patience for confirmation and she nodded.

"Come sit down. Jim, did you see him?"

"No."

"I *did* see him," Patience spoke for the first time, thinking the sheriff didn't believe her.

"I'm sure you did. Now, what was he wearing?"

"That big camouflage army coat, jeans and boots."

"A hat?"

"No, there's a hood on the coat."

"Was he clean-shaven?" the sheriff asked, studying Patience.

"No. He still had his beard. And those beady black eyes," she added, shuddering.

"I remember," the sheriff said.

Patience stared at him. "You've met him?"

"Yes. Jon called me when Faith died. Kane was outside the house when I arrived. He took one look at me and rushed away."

"I'm going to take Patience back to the ranch," Jim said. "Will you look around town for him?"

"I will. You two be careful out on the road by yourselves. He'll have heard where Patience and the boy are."

Jim pulled Patience to her feet. "We know."

Patience was trembling. Jim held her close and pulled his cell phone out of his coat pocket. He called his father. "Dad? Kane is in town. We're heading back now. Expect us soon."

He hung up and smiled at Patience. "Let's go."

BACK AT THE RANCH, Patience checked on Tommy, finding him playing with Davy. She pulled him into her arms and hugged him close.

"What's wrong, Mommy?" he asked.

She didn't want to alarm him. "Nothing. But I was gone a long time. I thought maybe you'd miss me."

"Sure," he said, kissing her cheek, but she knew he was agreeing just to make her happy.

Jim had followed her into the room.

"Hey, Tommy, I know your mom just got home, but I'm going to have to borrow her for a little while, okay?"

Tommy, of course, had no problem with this. Now he could get back to the game he and Davy were playing.

Patience didn't know what Jim's intentions were, but she patted Tommy on the head. "All right. I'll be back soon."

With so much on her mind, she didn't even question where she and Jim were headed. He handed her her coat and led the way out to the barn. "We're going there again so we can have some privacy," he said, watching to see if she'd object.

Patience had complete faith in Jim, however. She followed him without complaint.

Inside the barn, he closed the doors, sending the dogs, who'd followed them, back to guard duty.

"Are you sure they understand?" she asked.

"Oh, yeah. Maybe some of the younger dogs wouldn't if they didn't have the older ones. But they'll alert us the minute any stranger is around."

"But I'm a stranger," she pointed out.

"Not really. You're with me. That makes you okay."

Patience gave a brief smile, thinking how ironic his words were.

Jim stepped toward her. "I wanted—"

The howl of the dogs interrupted him. Quickly he moved Patience behind him and drew his gun.

Chapter Twelve

"He's here!" Patience gasped, clutching Jim's uninjured shoulder.

"We'll see," Jim said calmly. He moved toward the barn door. When he reached it, he said to Patience, "Stay here for just a minute."

"No! I want to go with you."

"You will. I'm not leaving you alone. But I want to take a look outside without risking you."

She took a step back, still staying in reach of Jim's broad shoulders.

"Jim?"

When he heard his father's voice, Jim relaxed. "We're in the barn."

"Just didn't want you to worry. A coyote got close. That's what alarmed the dogs, but you two should probably come back to the house."

"Yeah, Dad. We're coming."

He reached for Patience's hand and they stepped out, glad to see Chad and Pete standing on the porch, rifles at the ready, waiting for them.

"You're sure, Dad?" Jim asked.

"Well, I saw a coyote, and that's the direction the dogs were dying to go. If anyone else is out there, the dogs will let us know after the coyote moves away."

"Tommy?" Patience asked.

"He and Davy are still playing. Toby and Brett are with them now," Chad replied.

"Thank you," Patience murmured.

"I don't think you two should go out to the barn until things settle down, okay?"

"Okay," Patience readily agreed.

When they got back in the house, the men left her in the kitchen with Megan, B.J., Red and Mildred. Jim assured her they were just going to work out a strategy and she shouldn't worry.

The men had gone to Jake's office to confer. "Jim says Patience saw Kane in town today. Patience is to go nowhere on her own," Jake told them. "The children are not to play outside. I made a list here of your names and when you have guard duty." He gave them each a copy.

"Everyone must assume his guard duty no matter what, understood?"

While everyone else nodded, Jim said, "Uncle Jake, my name's not on the list."

"I know. You're still recovering and," he continued as Jim started to protest, "you're acting as Patience's personal guard. You stay with her no matter what."

Jim couldn't argue with that assignment. "I appreciate all this. Be careful. I don't want any of you hurt."

Chad gave him a hug. "We feel the same way. And we're not going to let this maniac mess things up for any of us."

Jim hoped his father was right.

He called the sheriff's office to see if he or his deputies had spotted Kane in town, but the sheriff said there was no sign of him.

Jim hung up and said, "Nothing."

Jake frowned. "Are you sure she actually saw him?"

"I don't know, Uncle Jake. I didn't see him, but her reaction was pretty strong. I believe her."

"Yeah. Well, we'll keep her safe here. And remember, no one goes anywhere alone. Okay?"

Drew grinned. "That's going to make scoring pretty hard on Friday night."

Chad frowned. "I'll speak with you in your bedroom, young man."

Drew, who'd thought they'd all laugh at his quip, looked alarmed. "I was just joking, Dad."

"This is not the time to joke, Drew," Chad said sternly.

"He knows it now, Dad," Jim said, championing his brother. Drew shot him a look of gratitude.

"Humph!" Chad grunted, still glaring at his son.

"Okay," Jake said, "anybody with night duty, you've got time to catch a nap now. Anybody on duty, man your posts. And don't say anything to the ladies."

Everyone but the four elder Randalls and Jim left the room. Jake clapped Chad on the shoulder. "Don't worry about Drew," he said. "He's just young."

"He's been out of university for six months now. It's about time he grew up," Chad growled.

The phone rang. Pete, closest to it, picked it up. "Randall Ranch."

"Jake's here. You want to talk to him?"

Pete handed the phone to Jake.

"Yeah? Oh, hi, Nick. Yeah. No, we're fine. We're prepared. No, you stay there and keep an eye on your family. The man is crazy. Thanks for offering. Call your brother Gabe and tell him not to come."

After a pause Jake said, "We will." Then he hung up the phone. "Nick and Gabe were going to come, but I convinced them to stay home. I'd better call Griff before he decides to come rescue us, too," he added, shaking his head.

"I'd better find Patience." Jim headed for the door.

"Boy?" Pete called.

"Yes, Uncle Pete?"

"You know you're hooked, don't you?"

Jim smiled. "Oh, yeah. I'm just waiting for things to settle." Then he headed in search of Patience, something he figured he'd be doing the rest of his life.

After consulting with Red, who always seemed to know where everyone was, Jim went to the spare room on the second floor that had been turned into a workout room. There was a thick carpet on the floor and weight machines along one wall.

When he peeked in, he saw his mother, B.J.

and Patience exercising to the beat of a popular tune. From his point of view, Patience didn't have any need for exercise. She was already in perfect shape, but she seemed happy to be working out.

The music ended and his mother noticed him watching. "Jim! Come on in. We're just finishing up."

"No hurry. I was enjoying the show," he replied, smiling at Patience.

Her cheeks were already flushed from the exercise, but they reddened even further at his look. She took the towel B.J. handed her and mopped her brow, glancing away from him.

"So, what's your plan?" Megan asked.

"My job is to keep an eye on Patience."

"But I'm safe, here in your house," Patience protested. "Even Kane wouldn't be crazy enough to try anything here."

"I would hope not," Jim agreed, "but we want to err on the side of caution. So, Patience, I'm keeping you company until we get rid of Joseph Kane."

"Things could be worse, Patience," B.J. said with a grin. "They could've assigned Red the task. Then you'd be stuck in the kitchen and he would keep feeding you!"

"Oh, my. That *would* be a problem," she agreed with a laugh.

Jim held out a hand. "Let's go check on the kids."

"I need to shower first," Patience said.

"Wow, this bodyguard job is gonna be tough," Jim said, his eyes dancing.

"Jim, don't tease Patience," his mother said. Then she turned to the young woman. "Dear, if he gives you any trouble, let me know at once. Even if he won't listen to me, he'll listen to his father."

"I always listen to you, Mom," Jim protested.

Megan ignored him. "Go take your shower, Patience. Jim will wait outside your door."

Patience swept past Jim and marched down the hallway. Her room was in the rear corner of the second floor. When they reached it, he opened the door and looked around. Waiting while she gathered her things for a shower, he walked her to the hall bathroom and checked it out, too.

"Okay, Princess, you're on your own." He sketched a bow and then leaned against the wall.

"Thank you," she said, refusing to play.

Jim tried to repress the desire he felt as she disappeared into the bathroom. His "duty" was going to be harder on him than one would think. He wanted to share *everything* with Patience. And his mind tempted him with images of her stripping naked for her shower....

He'd almost forgotten why he was there in the hallway when he was jolted by her scream. With no thought to her modesty, he burst into the small, steam-filled room.

"Patience! Are you all right? What's wrong?"

Patience grabbed a towel and covered herself. Then she confessed, "Nothing! I forgot about the coatrack. Through the shower curtain, it looked like a man and I thought..."

Jim turned and looked behind him. His mother, an interior designer by profession and with a shop in Rawhide, had decorated the bathroom. She'd put a coat rack in the bathroom, a tall coat rack that swiveled and stood in the corner so that whoever used the bath could hang their clothes on it.

Jim, once he understood the problem, ignored Patience's stumbling explanation and enjoyed the sight of her legs and shoulders glistening with water droplets and nothing else.

"I, uh, better let you get dressed," he said.

He moved slowly, finally closing the door on the glorious sight of her.

With a groan he collapsed against the wall, his mind's eye still tracing her body without the towel. He hoped he never forgot that sight. He figured it was going to be a long time before he could convince Patience of his love and have the chance to see her almost naked again.

Five minutes later she opened the door, sedately dressed in a long skirt and a knit top. Barefoot, she immediately began apologizing. "I shouldn't be so skittish, not with you right here to protect me, but it took me by surprise."

"Not a problem. I'd rather you sound the alarm any time you're unsure, rather than hold back until it's too late."

"I need to go back to my bedroom and get some shoes."

"Are you dressing up for dinner? You don't have to do that here, you know. We're casual."

"I know. But I like to wear a skirt sometimes. It's good to change from blue jeans now and then."

He followed her down the hall and couldn't help agreeing with her. When she stepped into the bedroom, she turned to close the door.

"If you're just getting ready, you know, doing

your hair and putting on shoes, I think it would be all right for me to come in.'' He waited for her response.

''I suppose so.''

She didn't sound enthusiastic, but he didn't hesitate to accept her offer as she held the door open. He sat down on the edge of her bed and watched her slip on some soft leather shoes. Then she sat at the vanity of the antique bedroom suite and began combing out her long hair.

''May I do that?''

Even Jim was surprised by his request. He hadn't planned it. But the desire to touch her in some way was almost overwhelming.

''It...it gets tangled. I don't think—''

He stood and took the comb from her cold hands. ''I'll be careful.'' He stood behind her and gently pulled the comb through the damp strands of blond hair. When he reached a tangle, he slowly picked it apart until the strands all flowed smoothly.

''Your hair is so beautiful,'' he told her softly. He regretted his words, however, because she opened her eyes wide, as if she'd been sleeping, and reached for the comb.

''Thank you. You've done a nice job of get-

ting rid of the tangles, but I need to dry it now.''
She reached for an electric dryer.

He didn't know if she expected him to leave
or not, but he returned to the bed and sat.

She stared at him. ''The dryer is noisy.''

''All the more reason for me to remain. I
might not hear anything over the sound.''

That appeared to make sense to her. She nodded and clicked on the dryer. Then she bent
over, turning her head upside down, and began
blowing dry the underside of her hair. After that,
she sat up and began smoothing down her hair
with a brush while she blew hot air on it.

''Do you do this every time you wash your
hair?'' Jim asked, fascinated with the process.

''No. After I comb it out, if I'm in a hurry, I
braid it and let it dry naturally. But when the
weather is cold, it's better to get it thoroughly
dry first.''

''I don't want you to braid it.''

She stared at him. ''Why not?''

''Because it's so beautiful loose. You didn't
used to braid it at school.''

She ignored his remark. ''It gets in my face
and I can't see to do any work. Now I'm going
to braid it, then go down to help with dinner.''

"Can't you wear a...a barrette or something?"

With a sigh, she said, "I'll only braid the front of it, okay?"

He watched her separate the hair around her face on each side and weave it into a braid about a pencil width. Then she circled that small braid into a coil and pinned it in place. When she finished, her hair was held back from her face, but the unbraided portion fell almost to her waist, a golden stream of hair that begged for his touch.

"You're beautiful," he said softly, rising to his feet.

"Jim! You mustn't say things like that."

"Why not?" he asked.

"Because it makes me think... I mean, I appreciate you guarding me, but that's all this is. You're playing a dangerous game when you say things like that. It makes me think you're...you know, like we used to be."

She jumped up and started for the door. But Jim couldn't let her go. He caught her and pulled her into his arms. "*I* am like we used to be, Patience, if by that you mean I love you. Because I do. I was going to wait until this thing with Kane is over, but you might as well know now that I love you."

He leaned down and kissed her with all the pent-up passion he'd been feeling. She stepped back, but she was unsteady as she stared at him, her eyes wide.

"You're just saying that because we've spent so much time together." Then she rushed from the room before he could move.

He'd known it was too soon to speak of his feelings, but he couldn't hold back. Now she'd made it plain she didn't want professions of love from him. And she'd probably ask for a change of guards if he continued to pursue her. Damn!

AFTER DINNER that evening, most of the younger Randalls moved in to the family room. There were lots of comfortable couches and chairs and a big-screen television.

Jim followed Patience in, even though he wasn't showing any enthusiasm.

Patience figured he'd already lost his enthusiasm for guarding her. But she'd tried to give him a break. All evening long, she'd stayed wherever the rest of the family was. He knew she was safe with his family.

But he'd stayed beside her, regardless.

However, there were no more amorous looks

or small touches. He was keeping everything strictly business.

Patience was glad. Of course she was. She didn't want him to feel obliged to court her. And that was what she was afraid was happening. The Randall parents watched them with a pleased eye. Red and Mildred treated them like honeymooners.

At least, that was how Patience interpreted those sly glances and secret smiles. So she avoided looking at Jim and left him to follow, never inviting him to stay close.

In the family room, she sat down with Elizabeth, Davy and Tommy. Elizabeth was saving the end seat for Toby.

"There's no room for me on this couch," Jim growled. "Let's move to the couch behind it."

"I'll be fine, Jim. You know I'm safe here." She shrugged.

"It's my job, Patience." He took her arm and helped her stand. "We'll be right behind Tommy."

With an apologetic smile at Elizabeth, Patience moved. However, she didn't snuggle up to Jim as Elizabeth did to Toby when he came in. He wrapped his arms around his wife and gave her a kiss.

A streak of jealousy shot through Patience. That was the kind of behavior she was trying to avoid—even though she'd love it. It wasn't fair to force Jim into a lover's role.

"Relax," he whispered in her ear. "I'm not going to attack you when the lights go down."

She wondered what he'd do if she said what she was thinking. She sighed and scooted away from him a little more.

The movie they were going to watch was a classic animated film the kids were sure to enjoy. Patience was glad. It would've been impossible to sit this close to Jim and watch a romance-themed movie.

When the movie began, she relaxed, carried away by the catchy music and the clever animation. She was also distracted by Tommy's reaction. He was clapping and laughing along with Davy. Steffie, in her mother's arms, seemed to like the movie, too. But halfway through it, Toby took his daughter from Elizabeth's arms and carried her up to bed, her head on her daddy's shoulder and her eyes closed.

Unconsciously Patience whispered, "Isn't she sweet?"

Suddenly she realized Jim's arm was around her. He gently pulled her against him and kissed the side of her head. "Yeah. Little girls always are."

He didn't release her when she tried to move away. And because it was what she secretly wanted, she settled back against him without protest.

When the movie ended, someone turned the lights on and Patience blinked in surprise. She straightened abruptly, leaving the warmth of Jim's arms. "Oh. That was a good movie. Did you like it, Tommy?" she asked, hoping to draw attention away from her and Jim.

"Shh," Elizabeth said. "Both boys are asleep."

"Oh! I didn't realize…"

Jim stood up. "I'll carry him up and help you undress him, Patience."

"Thank you. Next time I'll have him watch the movie in his pajamas," she said, smiling. Then she realized how presumptive that sounded. "I mean, if we…if there is a next time."

"There will be," Jim assured her, straightening with Tommy in his arms.

She didn't look at him until he'd gone past her, carrying her sweet little boy. She quietly followed him.

Upstairs they worked together to get Tommy into his pajamas and tucked into bed.

"Are you going to bed now, too?" Patience asked Jim as he walked her to her room.

"Maybe."

They'd reached her door. She paused, staring at Jim. "What do you mean, maybe?"

"I'm guarding you. I'll bed down out here so I can get to you quickly if you call out."

Patience sighed. "I'll be fine. I don't want you losing sleep. You need to recover from your wound."

"No argument, Patience. I'm guarding you."

Patience took a deep breath. "Then come inside." She turned and entered her room, not looking to see if he joined her.

Chapter Thirteen

When Patience reached her bed, she picked up her nightgown and headed for the bathroom. Jim stepped in front of her and grasped her arm.

"Wait a minute. What do you want me to do, exactly?"

She drew a breath, hoping she could be honest without pleading. "I…I want you to share my bed."

He stared at her but didn't release her. "Why?"

So he was going to force her to spell it out. Okay, she would. "I want you to make love to me, and I hope you want the same thing." Her voice was trembling by the time she finished, but she thought she'd made herself clear.

Jim swept her into his arms and kissed her, a long, deep kiss she felt all the way to her toes.

"You know I want to," he whispered when they came up for air. "But—"

Patience stopped his words by covering his mouth with her hand. "No, Jim, I don't want to discuss it. I always say the wrong thing. I won't hold you to anything right now. You're safe. Just…love me."

This time she kissed him, needing his touch now more than ever.

He smiled at her after their kiss and took her nightgown away from her. "You won't be needing this, honey." Then he began unbuttoning her knit top. She'd assumed she'd be horribly embarrassed, but she found she wasn't. This was Jim, and Jim was the right person, whatever happened. She began unbuttoning his shirt, too.

"Damn!"

Patience jerked her eyes open. "What's wrong?"

"I don't suppose you're on the Pill, are you?"

It took her a moment for his words to sink in. "Uh, no."

"Okay. I've got to go to my bedroom."

She moaned. How could he do this to her when she'd finally gotten up the nerve to tell him what she wanted?

He kissed her. "Not for the night, honey. I've

got to go get protection. It won't take but a couple of minutes.''

''Oh. Okay.'' She kept telling herself she was pleased that he'd thought of it. ''Sure. I'll wait here.''

He kissed her again quickly and backed out of her bedroom.

She only hoped he remembered to button his shirt before he went through the kitchen.

WHEN JIM RUSHED back up the stairs, after trying to appear calm as he strode through the kitchen, he found Patience's bedroom door closed.

What would he do if she'd changed her mind? He certainly hadn't. He rapped softly on the door. ''It's me,'' he said.

''Come in,'' her sweet voice called out. So far, so good. Jim opened the door to find the room darkened. ''Patience?'' he called, reaching for the lightswitch.

''No, Jim, don't turn on the light.''

''Why not?'' he asked as he approached the bed. In the shadows, he could see Patience in the bed, the covers drawn to her neck. ''Did you change your mind? If you did, I won't be angry. I know this is a difficult time for you.''

"I thought you wanted me."

"I do. Absolutely. But I don't want to force you or anything."

She threw back the covers, revealing her naked body. "Does this look like you have to force me?"

"Mercy," he muttered, and began tugging off his boots and unfastening his jeans as fast as he could.

She sat up and began unbuttoning his shirt again. In less than a minute, he was as naked as she was, and sliding under the covers, flesh against flesh.

He kissed her, his hands touching her everywhere. She loved the feel of him, the warmth of him and, most of all, his eagerness. Just when she thought she was going to explode, he stopped moving.

"Jim? What's wrong? Did I do something wrong?"

"Hardly," he told her, chuckling, "but my trip to get the condoms was a waste of time if we don't use them."

"Oh!"

He reached over her, found his jeans on the floor and fished a condom out of his pocket. After he'd prepared himself, he turned his complete attention back to Patience. Then he positioned himself over her, eager to become one with the only woman he'd ever loved.

As he pushed her legs apart and began his entry, something kept niggling in his mind. When he felt the initial resistance, he knew what it was. She was a virgin.

Patience almost whimpered his name. "Jim?"

"Honey, why didn't you say it was your first time?" He gritted his teeth.

"Because it doesn't matter. I want you!" she exclaimed. "Do you want me or not?"

"Of course I want you. There's no question of that."

"Then make love to me, please," she said quietly.

Jim gave up. They'd talk tomorrow, he assured himself, but he couldn't turn down what he wanted so badly. He built their momentum to fever-pitch again, to make it less painful for Patience. Then he pushed through.

She gasped, and he stroked her body, whispering sweet words in her ear. When she began to relax, he started moving, creating a rhythm that seemed to explode between them only a few minutes later.

He removed the condom and deposited it in the wastebasket beside the bed. Then he cuddled

Patience in his arms, remembering their night in the cabin. "Patience?" he whispered.

"Just hold me, Jim. Just hold me," she pleaded as she pressed against him.

That he could do. In fact, he intended to do so for the rest of their lives. He'd tell her so tomorrow.

THEY'D MADE LOVE again a couple of hours after the first time. Again, as Patience had requested, there'd been no conversation. Afterwards they'd fallen asleep in each other's arms.

When Jim awoke the next morning, it was very early. But he'd slept better than he had for months. He grinned. No wonder. He'd made love to Patience. He'd like to wake her now and make love again, but he'd only brought two condoms to her room last night.

He'd better concentrate on getting to the bachelor pad and taking a shower before the rest of the house was up. He had about fifteen minutes before Red appeared in the kitchen.

He quietly dressed, forcing himself to leave without kissing Patience. He didn't want to disturb her sleep when there was nothing he could do about it.

Half an hour later, he entered the kitchen and

filled a mug of the coffee Red had brewed. "Morning, Red."

"Morning, boy. Patience okay?"

"Yeah, she's fine." Jim didn't meet his gaze.

"How about I fix her breakfast and you can carry a tray up?"

"Good idea. She might be tired. All this stress can get to a person." Jim hoped Red prepared a tray soon. He'd rather not face his father this morning. Not until he'd had a chance to talk to Patience.

When Drew and Josh came in, Jim realized they were coming off guard duty. "Any problems last night?" he asked.

"Nope," Drew replied. "It was so quiet we had trouble staying awake."

"Good. I hope Kane's given up and gone away." Now that he and Patience were together again, he could almost forgive Joseph Kane for his crazy behavior. Without it, he might still be sitting here miserable and alone, with a big chip on his shoulder.

Instead, he'd held Patience all night long, just as he'd dreamed.

"Look at him," Drew said, poking Josh. "We lost a lot of sleep and he's sitting there grinning like the cat that swallowed the canary."

Jim wiped the smile from his face. "Sorry, I was thinking of something else."

"Here's the girl's tray, Jim," Red said. "Get it up to her before it gets cold."

Delighted with Red's timing, Jim nodded to his brother and cousin and, grabbing the tray, beat a retreat. As he climbed the stairs, he noticed that Red had included a second cup of coffee for him.

He didn't bother to knock on the door. He expected Patience to still be sleeping in the big bed they'd shared. He shut the door behind him and turned to the bed, a smile on his face.

The bed was empty.

He hurriedly set down the tray and scooted to the bathroom down the hall. Knocking on the door, he quietly called, "Patience?"

"Yes?"

Relief filled him. "I've got a breakfast tray for you in the bedroom."

She didn't respond. "Patience, did you hear me?" he asked.

"Yes. But take it back downstairs. I'll be down in a minute."

"But, honey, I thought we could talk about last night. You know, have a little privacy."

She yanked open the door, a frown on her face. "I told you last night I didn't want to discuss it. I still don't. I'll get the tray.'' She tried to brush past him.

Hurt by her behavior, Jim held her back. ''I'll get the damned tray. You can skitter down the stairs to safety!'' He was practically shouting by the time he finished.

''Thank you,'' she said coolly, and walked past him.

He stood there, boiling mad that she could dismiss their lovemaking as she had. Was she through with him? The thought almost stopped his heart.

He went back to her room and picked up the tray, his movements so hurried that the coffee slopped on to the tray. He reached the kitchen in time to hear her say to Red, ''You don't need to wait on me. I'll take my breakfast with everyone else.''

''We start early around here,'' Red warned.

''Tommy does, too. I'm used to early hours.''

Patience then sat down beside Drew and began talking to him.

Jim frowned at her. What was she doing? He set the tray down hard, spilling more coffee, and set the full plate of food in front of her. ''I'll refill the mugs,'' he muttered. He took the tray to the sink and poured off the spilled coffee, then topped off the mugs. He almost spilled them again when he turned and saw Patience laugh at something Drew said and reach out to lightly tap his arm.

"Jim! Be careful or you're gonna scald yourself," Red warned.

"Yeah," Jim muttered as he reached the table and sat down on Patience's other side.

"Haven't you eaten already?" she asked.

"Yeah. What's it to you?" he growled.

Drew stared at him. "Wow, that was quick. Five minutes ago you were smiling to beat the band. Now you sound like a real sourpuss. What happened?"

"Mind your own business," Jim growled, not looking at Patience or his brother.

After Patience finished her breakfast and put her dishes in the dishwasher, she left the kitchen to go check on Tommy. Jim followed her. "Wait a minute."

She turned to look at him. "What?"

"I don't know what kind of game you're playing, but don't flirt with Drew. That's not fair!"

"Flirt with Drew? Don't be ridiculous. I was just talking to him."

"Yeah, right!" He wasn't buying it.

"Morning," Megan called as she came down the stairs. "Everything okay this morning?"

"Yes, fine," Patience assured her as she stepped aside. "I'm just going up to check on Tommy."

"I think Elizabeth is doing the same thing. I heard voices in the boys' bedroom."

"Oh, I'd better hurry. I don't want to give her double duty." With a smile, Patience hurried up the stairs.

Jim stood there, staring after her as if someone had stolen his favorite toy.

"What's wrong, son?"

"Uh, nothing, Mom. I was just wondering if I needed to follow. I'm not moving as fast as usual, you know."

"Come have some coffee with me. I'm sure Davy and Tommy will be down to breakfast soon. I don't want you overdoing things."

The rest of the day followed the same pattern. Patience avoided being alone with him at every turn. He tried to figure out what she was thinking. He even asked his father in a roundabout way, but Chad only shrugged. "Better ask your mother. Women are hard to figure out."

Jim had no intention of approaching his mother. She'd have all his secrets out of him in no time. She was good at that.

When Tommy went down for his afternoon

nap, Jim caught Patience in the hallway alone. "What are you—"

She broke in with, "You'd better go gather some of your things and put them in my room, so you don't have to run back and forth every day."

He stared at her, stunned by the implications of her words. She pulled from his hold and continued on down the stairs.

By the time he collected himself, she was out of sight. It took him only a couple of minutes to decide to do as she suggested. He wasn't strong enough to resist making love to her tonight if that was what she wanted. So he'd get some clothes and every condom he had, and move them to her room.

That night, she went up to bed when he was speaking with his father, and it took him a few minutes to get free. He hurried upstairs as fast as he could, anxious to discover if she'd meant what she'd implied earlier.

When he opened the door, the light was again off and Patience was in bed.

He gulped and cleared his throat. "Do you want me to stay here with you?"

"Yes, of course," she agreed calmly, reaching a bare arm toward him.

He abandoned his clothing in a flash and

joined her under the covers as he had the previous night. The condoms he'd left on the bedside table were quite handy…fortunately.

The next morning, he didn't worry about disturbing Patience's sleep. He kissed her awake and they made love in the early-morning light. He couldn't think of a better way to start the day.

After he rolled off her, he leaned over and kissed her lips again. "Good morning."

"Morning," Patience said, but she was already trying to slide out of bed.

"Wait a minute, honey," he said, catching her arm. "We need to talk."

"No, we don't. I told you I don't want to talk."

"But we can't continue like this," he protested, wanting to explain his plans for the future.

She misinterpreted his meaning. "If you don't want to sleep with me, Jim, stop climbing into bed with me." Then she stood and pulled on her robe. Before he could recover from the surprise and the pleasure of seeing her nude again, she was out the door and headed for the bathroom.

What was wrong with her? Why was she acting as if what they did at night had no meaning?

He knew she hadn't behaved like this in the

past. Not with him, not with anyone. So what was going on?

When she returned from her shower, she told him he'd better hurry if he wanted to use the bathroom. She thought her mother would be heading there in a few minutes.

He was out the door at once. Then he remembered Mrs. Anderson's saying yesterday that she didn't get up until around eight. Patience had suckered him into rushing into the bathroom so she could go downstairs without him.

When he went downstairs, she and Elizabeth were taking care of the children, and she declined his assistance.

And that was how the entire day went. By the time he went upstairs after her that night, he'd given up trying to talk to her. But he couldn't give up making love to her. Again she welcomed him to her bed and enthusiastically participated in the lovemaking.

He decided she had some kind of plan that she didn't want to share with him. But as long as she let him make love to her, he didn't think he had the energy to resist.

The next morning, however, when they were both having breakfast with his parents, she announced she was going into town.

"What?" Jim demanded at once, noting the surprise on all the other adults' faces, too.

"I'm going to town. I need to check on the house. And get my gun. The waiting period is over."

"But Patience," Chad said, watching both her and Jim, "I don't think it's safe yet."

"Mr. Randall, I appreciate everyone's hospitality and sacrifice, but it can't go on forever. There's been no sign of Kane—I think I must have imagined seeing him. It's time to get Tommy's life and mine back on track. Besides, I'll be getting custody of Tommy soon, and Kane will have to leave us alone."

Jim considered arguing with her, but he decided to do that later. Right now he needed to ensure she spent her day safely. "I'll go with you," he said, his voice like steel.

Chapter Fourteen

Patience's car hadn't been started for several days and it took a minute to warm up. "Good thing I wasn't trying to make a fast exit."

"Seems to me your exit was pretty fast as it was." Jim stared straight ahead.

She shifted into reverse and began backing up. Her little car was parked between two large trucks. She shifted into first and headed down the long driveway.

"I've leaned on your family for too long already. Besides, there's obviously no danger. No one has seen or heard from Kane since we came down from the mountains."

"What about your seeing him in town?"

Patience shrugged. "I think I just panicked because someone resembled Kane. If it *had* been him, he would've made his move by now."

"What if you're wrong?" Jim still stared straight ahead, his voice cold.

Patience mentally compared the warm, loving man she'd spent the night with to the angry man beside her now. She wanted to be able to fall into his arms and leave her safety up to him. But she couldn't. And the nights spent in his arms were making her weak.

She had to protect her family. That was her job. And she couldn't make Jim responsible for her and Tommy just because she'd slept with him. He'd believe forever that she had purposely trapped him. Which was why she had to end her stay at the Randall Ranch.

Because she also had to end her affair with Jim.

Slowly, each word measured, she said, "If I'm wrong, I'll be the only one hurt."

"And Tommy?"

"I…I want to ask a favor, Jim. If something happens to me, would you keep an eye on Tommy?"

"Pull over!" Jim snapped.

She eased the car to a halt on the side of the county road. "Yes?"

"Don't you know how much it would hurt me if anything happened to you?"

Now it was her turn to stare straight ahead. She couldn't face him.

When she didn't respond, Jim grabbed her shoulders and turned her toward him. "Patience, what's going on? You know I love you!"

"No, I don't," she said, trying to twist free.

Jim withdrew his hands. "What?"

"I know you like to have sex with me. That's all I know."

"Because you kept telling me you didn't want to talk. I don't understand what you're doing, but that doesn't mean I don't love you."

"Jim, we had…sex because we both wanted it. That's all. I wasn't trying to trick you into marriage. I didn't ask for a proposal before I'd sleep with you."

Jim was confused. "What are you saying?"

"Nothing. I'm saying nothing, and I don't intend to spend the day on the side of the road involved in a meaningless discussion." She put her car in gear and drove on toward Rawhide.

After several minutes of silence Jim asked, "So you just wanted sex? That's all?"

"Isn't that what you wanted three years ago?"

Jim squared his jaw. How could he answer her? "Look, Patience, I was young and stupid.

I didn't like anyone forcing my hand. But I loved you then. I love you now.''

"Don't! I didn't ask for any promises.'' She parked by the gun store and got out of the car. "I have to pick up my gun.''

Jim sat there, staring as she marched into the gun shop. He didn't know what to do. Finally he decided to go visit the sheriff, whose office was just across the street. He'd be able to keep an eye on Patience through the window.

With a sigh, Jim headed into the sheriff's office. There was little activity there. Several deputies were at their desks doing paperwork. The sheriff was in his office on the phone. One of the deputies looked up.

"Hello, Jim. What's up?''

"I just wanted to know if there'd been any sign of Joseph Kane.''

The deputy shook his head. "We've been on the lookout. We stopped one guy who matched Patience's description of Kane, but he had ID on him. His name was Charles Johnson.''

"Why didn't you call us?'' Jim asked.

"No reason to. I told you, it wasn't Kane. Mr. Johnson explained that he bought the coat for ten dollars from a man heading south. He even found some of those fake coins in the pocket. He gave them to me.''

"How considerate of him," Jim returned sarcastically.

"No need to get testy, Jim."

"Look, just tell the sheriff that Patience and I are going to be over at her house today. He can call us there if anything comes up."

Jim headed back across the street just as Patience came out of the gun store. "Get in the car," he said. "I don't want you standing around in public."

"Jim, you're being overprotective."

"One of the deputies told me they stopped a guy they thought looked like Kane—he was wearing that jacket you described. He said he bought it off a guy who was heading south." He watched her, waiting to see her reaction.

Alarm flashed in her eyes. "Did they check this guy's ID?"

"Yeah. His name was Charles Johnson." Jim drew a deep breath. "I don't like the sound of it."

She slid behind the wheel of her car. "So maybe Kane *has* left town."

"This guy seemed a little too helpful to be real. He had an answer for anything they wanted to know." Jim frowned, still thinking about the deputy's words. "He even showed them some of those weird coins Kane had. Said they'd been left in the pocket of the coat."

"Maybe they found them when they searched him."

"The deputy didn't mention searching him. I guess he thought there was no need because the man was so forthcoming. That's what bothers me." He gave Patience a long, hard stare. "I don't think you should move back into town yet."

She wiped away anything in her expression that might make him think she agreed with him. "And how long should I stay there? Another week? Another month? No, Jim. It's time we moved back."

"I think your mother should've named you stubborn, instead of Patience."

Jim sighed. She was determined to get the house ready today. He guessed they could do that. Then he'd get his parents to talk her into staying another few days. He'd take things a little at a time and would eventually persuade her never to leave.

They reached Patience's home and parked in front. Jim took a good look at the house. It didn't appear disturbed. There were houses and neighbors on both sides. Surely they would've reported any disturbance to the sheriff.

"You go on in," he ordered, wanting her out of sight quickly. "I'll bring in the gun." He watched as she unlocked the front door and disappeared inside.

Jim picked up the gun and bag of accessories from the gun shop and carried it into the kitchen. He noted that Patience must have gone into her bedroom, so when the phone rang, he yelled, "I'll get it." Lifting the receiver he said, "Anderson's."

"Jim? This is the sheriff. My deputy told me you were at Patience's. The owner of the sandwich place just came in to complain about a customer using those fake coins for his meal."

"When?" Jim demanded, panic building in him.

"The guy went into the shop yesterday. The owner didn't get around to mentioning it until today. The description sounds like Joseph Kane, but he's shaved off his beard. Still has a mustache, though."

"Damn! Okay, thanks for letting me know."

"Listen, I already called your dad to let him know about the situation. He said to tell you he's on his way. He'll come to Patience's house. Should I come talk to her? He said she's determined to move back in tomorrow, and I don't think that's a good idea.''

''Yes. That might be wise.''

''I'll be over in a few minutes,'' the sheriff said.

Jim hung up. Patience still hadn't come out of her room. He called her name. Loudly.

''Jimmy? Can you come here please?''

Two things bothered him. Her voice didn't sound right. And she'd called him Jimmy. She never called him Jimmy. She only used Jimmy when she was scared or stressed.

Jim took off his holster and withdrew his gun. Then he shoved it into the back of the waistband of his jeans, so he'd appear unarmed. ''Okay,'' he called, keeping his voice calm, ''I'm coming.'' He moved down the short hallway until he reached the one door that was closed.

He grabbed the doorknob and quickly opened it.

PATIENCE WAS DISTURBED that coming home didn't feel as good as it should have. She had to come home now. She had to assume control of her life. It was bad enough that she'd slept with

Jim, making the leaving all the more difficult. She couldn't continue to rely on him.

Moving down the hall, she pushed open the door to her room. This room had been her sanctum, her place to hide from the world. But it felt different today. Maybe it was—

Cold steel pressed against her temple and an arm held her in place.

"Hello, Patience," Kane greeted her. "It took you a while to come home, didn't it? I've been waiting none too patiently."

"What are you doing here?" she demanded, her voice tight with fear.

"Taking my revenge. You destroyed my plans. And then there's the issue of my son."

"You'll be breaking the law. I'm going to be named Tommy's legal guardian. If you try to take him again, the police will arrest you."

He just laughed. Just then the phone rang. She tried to pull from his hold and answer it, but he held her firmly.

"Oh, no, my dear. You will not talk to anyone."

Then she heard Jim announce that he'd get it.

"Ah. So the stranger who betrayed me is here. Good. That will make it easy for me to take my revenge."

"No! It's not Jim's fault. I forced him to help me."

"Then he's a weak man to be ruled by a woman."

"Please don't hurt him!"

"You'd better worry about what's going to happen to you, Patience. You ran away rather than accept my proposal. So you are of no use to me, unless you've changed your mind."

She knew what she needed to say to live, but she couldn't. She couldn't even bear the thought of this man touching her as Jim had done. Not even to save her life. "No. I haven't changed my mind."

"Patience?"

The muzzle of the gun jammed harder against her temple. "Tell him to come here."

Frantically Patience tried to think of a way out. At last she called, "Jimmy, can you come here, please?"

She held her breath as she heard Jim move down the hall as if everything was normal.

Jim opened the door and stepped inside. Patience immediately noticed that he wasn't wearing the gun he'd had on earlier.

"Hands up, dear Jim," Kane said with a sneer. "I'm going to put you out of your misery soon enough, but first I intend to gloat a little. You thought you'd beaten me, didn't you? But I cannot be beaten. God owes me!'' His voice had changed to a roar.

"Is that so? Well, if you're so invincible, unhand Patience. Surely you don't need *her*."

"No, I don't. But I have no intention of turning her loose. She's my shield. Where is the boy?''

"He's safe," Jim replied.

"I want him! Go get him, and I'll keep Patience alive long enough to say goodbye," Kane said arrogantly.

"No. I won't go get the boy and I won't leave Patience alone with you."

"Jim, go! You can keep Tommy safe…and yourself." Patience felt tears in her eyes, but she fought to keep them from falling.

Jim smiled at her. "No, honey, that's not the way it works. You've already told me you mean to kill her, anyway. So I would gain nothing by doing as you ask."

"Save Tommy, Jim, please," Patience cried.

Before she knew what was happening, Kane spun her away from him and slapped her. "He'll do as I say!" Kane shouted.

At the same time, Jim crouched down, drew his pistol from behind his back and fired.

Kane fell to his knees. His blood spattered Patience and she screamed.

From outside came a shout and the sound of running boots.

Jim reached Patience just before his father and the sheriff appeared in the doorway.

Mass confusion reigned for a few minutes. In all the commotion, Kane, bleeding and on the floor, reached out for the gun that had fallen from his hand. Patience saw the movement and screamed just as another shot rang out. Kane's lifeless body slumped to the floor.

She looked up to see the sheriff with his gun drawn, staring at Kane. Chad looked at the two of them and asked, "Are you all right?"

Jim nodded. "We are. Patience is strong. She'll be okay."

She shuddered against him. She hoped he was right. She had to be.

Chapter Fifteen

The sheriff holstered his gun and pulled out a cell phone to summon his deputies to take care of the body.

Chad looked at Jim and Patience. "Son, why don't you take her back to the ranch?"

"Okay, Dad. Thanks for being here for us."

"Glad I could help. But the sheriff is the one who ended it. Everything is going to be fine now. Tell your mom I'll be home shortly."

Jim wrapped his arm around Patience and led her to the kitchen. There he picked up her coat and helped her put it on. Then he grabbed his own coat and headed for Patience's car.

"How about I drive, honey?"

She nodded, but didn't speak. She was afraid she'd start crying. She handed him the keys from her coat pocket and got in the passenger side.

Jim leaned down and dropped a kiss on her pale lips. Then he closed the door and circled the car to climb in behind the wheel.

They made the drive in silence. She knew he'd turned to look at her several times, but she couldn't chance catching his look of concern, afraid it might break her control. She closed her eyes and said nothing.

When they reached the ranch, Red met them at the back door.

"Did you see your dad? He was going to meet—"

"Yeah, Red, we saw him. Everything's over. Kane is dead and..."

Patience pulled free of his grasp and ran through the kitchen and up the stairs to her room. She needed to be alone to deal with what had happened.

JIM STOOD THERE in the middle of the kitchen and watched Patience's retreat.

"Did I say something wrong?" Red asked anxiously.

"No, Red, you didn't." With a sigh Jim explained what had happened at the Anderson house.

"Lord have mercy. That poor girl."

"I know. I think she needs some time alone."

Megan came into the kitchen. "Jim! I thought I heard Patience's car." She looked around the room. "Where is she?"

Jim shrugged. "She went up to her room. She…she had a difficult time today."

"Where's your dad?" Megan asked, anxiety in her voice.

"He's fine, Mom. Kane is dead. Dad stayed in town to help the sheriff deal with everything."

B.J. entered the kitchen in the middle of Jim's explanation. She put her arm around Megan but said nothing.

"Who shot him?" Megan asked.

"I shot him first. He was holding Patience with a gun to her head. Then he lost his temper and struck her. As she fell to the floor, I drew my gun and shot him. He was still alive and went for his gun again. The sheriff finished him off."

"I'm glad it's over," B.J. said. "I'm going to call Jake. He'll be relieved to hear the news. Where is Patience?"

"She went to her room."

"She's not hurt?" Megan asked.

"I suspect she'll have a bruise on her cheek, and she may be a little sore tomorrow, but that's all. Where are the boys?" he asked.

"In the game room of course," Megan said. "I think they're spending too much time playing video games, but we didn't want them outside. Maybe I should tell them they can go out."

"I'll do it. I'll get them to go with me and help do the feeding. It'll be good for them."

He left the kitchen and headed for the game room. As his mother had said, the boys were zealously playing their video games. "Davy, Tommy, it's okay for you to go outside again. Want to come help me feed the animals? We can get it all done before the guys come in. That way they won't have to do it before they come home."

"Okay!" Davy said, standing up. "That means I'll see my daddy sooner."

"That's right, Davy. How about you, Tommy?"

"Mommy said I had to stay inside."

"I know she did, but everything's okay now. You're safe. Your, uh…that mean man has gone away. He won't bother you anymore," Jim told him.

He made sure the boys were warmly dressed and led them to the first barn, where a few animals were stabled. He let the boys help him, though he did the lion's share of the work. The activity felt good.

About halfway through, Chad joined them.

"I can get it, Dad," Jim assured him.

"I'm sure you can. How's Patience?"

"I think she's okay. She's resting right now."

They finished the feeding just as the other Randall men arrived home. They were pleased to find the chores already done. As Chad gave them a brief summary of the day's events, Jim hurried the two boys to the house, taking them to the bathroom to wash up.

"That was fun, Jim," Tommy said as he washed his hands.

"I'm glad. We're going to need to get you a horse pretty soon. Once you learn to ride, maybe we can take your mommy on a picnic next spring. That's always fun."

"I have a horse," Davy said.

"I want a horse," Tommy said earnestly, "but Mommy said my room isn't big enough."

Jim laughed. "Well, horses don't live in houses. Maybe we can find a place for him here."

"But then I couldn't see him."

Jim picked up the little boy. "Maybe we'll talk your mommy into living here with me, and you can come, too. Then you could see the horse every day."

"Yea! And I could see Davy, too."

"Right. And Steffie."

"Oh, yeah, but she's a girl."

"Yeah," Davy seconded.

"When you get older, you'll find out how important girls are." Jim hoped he could convince Patience of that. "Okay, you two go down to dinner. I'm going to check on your mother, Tommy. We'll be down in a few minutes."

He watched the two boys go down the stairs, smiling as they discussed what Tommy would name his horse.

He walked down the long hall to Patience's bedroom. He couldn't help but think about the conversation they'd had earlier that day about the things that had been happening each night. She hadn't forgiven him for his youthful blunder in college. Not that he blamed her, but he wished she could.

Knocking on the door, he waited for her to respond. But he heard nothing. Slowly he opened the door. The room was almost dark, lit only by the setting sun.

He walked softly to the side of the bed, staring down at her sweetly curved body under the covers. He sat down and gently shook her shoulder. "Patience?"

Her eyes fluttered open, then closed again.

"Patience, it's dinnertime, honey. Do you want to come downstairs?"

She opened her eyes and pushed herself up, the blanket falling to her waist. She was wearing only her underwear. "I—I'm sorry you were involved in what happened today."

"I'm not," he said. "I'm glad it was the sheriff's shot that killed him, though, and not mine, and I'm glad Kane is gone forever."

"Yes," she said quietly.

"I took the boys out with me to feed the animals. They had a good time."

"I guess they would. Tommy likes to be outside."

"Yeah." He coughed before he said, "I, uh, promised him a horse."

She stared at him in shock. "You what? How could you do such a thing? We don't have a place for a horse. He'll be so disappointed!"

Jim took hold of her shoulders, giving her a little shake. "When we're married and living here on the ranch, of course he'll need a horse."

She looked away. "That's not going to happen."

"Yes, it is! We love each other."

"I don't remember saying I love you. You just feel guilty because I saved your life."

"Today I saved your life, didn't I?"

"Yes."

"And you saved mine. That makes us even, right?"

She nodded cautiously, not sure where he was going with this logic.

"You've already said we slept together because we both wanted it."

"Jim, I don't know—"

"Right?"

"Yes, but I've changed my mind."

"About what?"

"About…having an affair," she said, suddenly realizing she was not dressed. She pulled up the covers.

"You didn't enjoy it?"

"Yes, but…I have a son. I can't be so irresponsible."

"I agree. That's why we should get married."

"Jim, I told you I didn't ask for any promises. It's not necessary." She tried to get out of bed.

"Sweetheart, how many times do I need to tell you I love you? I've loved you for quite a while. And now that I've tasted life with you, I can't go back to life without you."

"But if I marry you, one day you'll claim I trapped you," she told him.

He took hold of her chin and turned her face toward him. "And I'll be giving thanks every time. I'm so glad you asked me for help and so glad I was smart enough to follow you up that mountain. Honey, I've loved you since college. I've never found anyone who could compare to you. I love you. We're perfect together.'' He kissed her. Then he said, ''We Randall men are one-woman guys. And you're my one woman.''

She shook her head. ''You're just saying that because you think you ought to. A month or two from now you'll realize you don't mean it.''

''How long?''

She blinked several times. Then she asked, ''How long what? What are you asking?''

''How long will it take for you to believe I want to be married to you?''

''Jim, stop being ridiculous.''

''I'm not. I want to know how long I have to wait until I can claim you for my wife. A wife I'm going to keep for the rest of my life.''

Tears began running down her cheeks. ''Jim, don't.''

''I have to, honey. I can't live without you in my life. I'll be Tommy's daddy. Your mother can live with us. We'll have a great life.''

''Do you promise you'll never regret marrying me?''

''I promise.''

She gave a big sigh. "Then I have to take the chance, because I'm miserable without you."

It took him a couple of seconds to realize she'd just accepted his offer. With a big cowboy whoop, he wrapped his arms around her and kissed her. When he came up for air, his first question was, "When?"

"I don't know. I suppose we'll have to consult our families."

"We can be married in three days. We'll go tomorrow and get the license in Buffalo."

"Three days? That's too soon. I want a real wedding!" she protested. "I'm only planning on having one."

Jim grinned. "Okay, I'll give you a week." He kissed her again. "Let's go down and tell everyone."

Downstairs the younger Randalls were finishing their meal and the older Randalls were gathering to take their turn at dinner.

Jim and Patience, holding hands, came into the kitchen. Jim was beaming and Patience looked a little embarrassed. "We're going to be married," Jim announced.

Everyone congratulated them. Tommy stared at them. "What's that mean?"

Jim squatted down beside the bench where Tommy sat. "It means you and your mommy, and Grandma, too, if she wants, are going to live with me. And you'll be my little boy.''

"I can call you Daddy? I've never had a daddy.''

"You can call me Daddy,'' Jim assured him. "Your name will be Tommy Randall, and Davy and Steffie will be your cousins.''

Tommy cheered the loudest of all.

"Have you set a date?'' Mrs. Anderson asked.

Jim and Patience gazed at each other. "Well,'' Jim said slowly, "I voted for three days from now, but Patience wants a real wedding, with a big cake and a reception. I agreed to a week from today.''

"Jim!'' Megan protested. "I don't know if we can get everything ready. Besides, a week from today would be Wednesday. Why not have the wedding a week from Saturday?''

Jim looked at Patience. "Is that okay with you?''

She nodded, her face glowing with pleasure.

Red immediately started making his famous chocolate cake to celebrate the announcement. Elizabeth volunteered her wedding gown for Patience to wear. Mildred and Red assured them they could make the wedding cake and all the food needed for the reception. The men said they'd clean the arena in case the weather was bad.

Patience stared around her in amazement. "I don't know what to say. It's so wonderful that everyone is pitching in."

"That's the Randall way," Jim told her.

Chad asked, "Where are you going to live?"

"I guess we'll start out in town," Jim said, "but I'd like to build a place out here."

"I have an idea," Red said. "Mildred and I have been talking about moving from our place down the road, back into the bedroom behind the kitchen," he said. "It's too hard to keep two houses clean and running."

"Are you sure, Red? Don't uproot yourselves just for our sake. We want you to be comfortable," Jim said.

"We're sure. We've talked about it a lot, but we hated to leave our little house empty. It's not huge, Jim, but it's got three bedrooms."

Jim looked at Patience. She gave a nod of approval.

"We'd love it, Red. Is that okay with you, Mrs. Anderson?"

She looked at the both of them. "I'd rather stay here where Mildred is going to live."

Jim hurriedly assured her the house was just a few steps away. Jake, however, intervened.

"We'd be glad to have you stay where you are, Marilyn, if it pleases you."

"Oh, thank you."

"Mom, are you sure?" Patience asked.

"Quite sure, dear. I love both you and Tommy, but sometimes the house is too noisy with all of us in it."

No one mentioned the crowd in the Randall household.

"What are you going to do with your house, Marilyn?" B.J. asked.

"I suppose we'll sell it."

B.J. looked at Jake. "I think it might be perfect for Caroline," she said, meaning her daughter who was due back in Rawhide soon.

Jake frowned. "Why can't she live at home?"

"She'll need to be close to the clinic," B.J. said. "Like Jon is."

"Okay. We'll buy it. Will that be okay with you, Marilyn?"

"Oh, yes."

Jake smiled at her. "Okay. Right now, though, we want to concentrate on your wedding. Welcome to the family, Patience." Jake stepped over and kissed her cheek. All the adults of the family followed suit.

Patience was overwhelmed. Then Jim's arms

came around her and she felt at peace. She was where she wanted to be.

''You sure you don't want to wait until Christmas when Caroline will be home?'' Jake asked.

Patience started to agree to wait, but Jim answered first. ''No! I'm not waiting any longer than I have to. I want to claim Patience and Tommy as mine as soon as possible.''

Jake lifted his glass and everyone else did likewise. ''A toast to Jim and Patience. May their marriage be long and happy and produce more grandchildren!''

Jim couldn't agree more.

* * * * *

Caroline Randall's story is next. Be sure to look for Judy Christenberry's
A RANDALL RETURNS,
available December 2003
from Harlequin American Romance.

HARLEQUIN®
INTRIGUE®

is proud to present
a chilling new trilogy
from beloved author

DANI SINCLAIR

**Behind the old mansion's closed door,
dark secrets lurk—
and deeper passions lie in wait.**

THE FIRSTBORN
(October)

THE SECOND SISTER
(November)

THE THIRD TWIN
(December)

Pick up all three stories in this dramatic family saga.
Available wherever Harlequin books are sold.

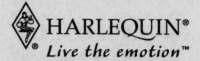

HARLEQUIN®
Live the emotion™

**Visit us at www.eHarlequin.com
and www.tryintrigue.com**

HIHEARTAMJ

Harlequin Romance®

**is proud to present a brand-new miniseries
from international bestselling author**

MARGARET WAY

**Come to Koomera Crossing,
deep in the Australian Outback....**

Experience the rush of love as these rich, rugged
bachelors meet their match—in the heart of Australia!

**October 2003—RUNAWAY WIFE #3767
November 2003—OUTBACK BRIDEGROOM #3771
December 2003—OUTBACK SURRENDER #3775**

*Don't miss this wonderful, passionate and exciting
miniseries, coming soon in Harlequin Romance*®*!*

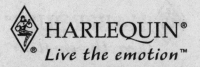

HARLEQUIN®
INTRIGUE®

has a new lineup of books to keep you on
the edge of your seat throughout the winter.
So be on the alert for...

BACHELORS AT LARGE

Bold and brash—these men have sworn to serve
and protect as officers of the law...and only the
most special women can "catch" these good guys!

UNDER HIS PROTECTION
BY AMY J. FETZER
(October 2003)

UNMARKED MAN
BY DARLENE SCALERA
(November 2003)

BOYS IN BLUE
A special 3-in-1 volume with
REBECCA YORK (Ruth Glick writing as Rebecca York),
ANN VOSS PETERSON AND PATRICIA ROSEMOOR
(December 2003)

CONCEALED WEAPON
BY SUSAN PETERSON
(January 2004)

GUARDIAN OF HER HEART
BY LINDA O. JOHNSTON
(February 2004)

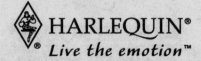

HARLEQUIN®
Live the emotion™

**Visit us at www.eHarlequin.com
and www.tryintrigue.com**

HIBBONTS

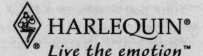

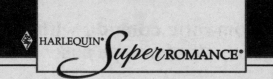

It's romantic comedy with a kick
(in a pair of strappy pink heels)!

Introducing

HARLEQUIN®
flipside

"It's chick-lit with the romance and happily-ever-after ending that Harlequin is known for."
—*USA TODAY* bestselling author Millie Criswell, author of *Staying Single*, October 2003

"Even though our heroine may take a few false steps while finding her way, she does it with wit and humor."
—Dorien Kelly, author of *Do-Over*, November 2003

Launching October 2003.
Make sure you pick one up!

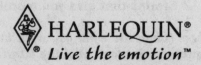

HARLEQUIN®
Live the emotion™

Visit us at www.harlequinflipside.com

HFGENERIC